ISLAND CONNECTION

Shared by the descendants – Jean, Joan, and Joyce McGinnis

Written by Jean's daughter, Kerrin Margiano

The spoken words revealing the stories related to the Money Pit have been handed down through the generations to us, and now to you.

ISBN 978-1533042392

Library of Congress Control Number: 2016907843
CreateSpace Independent Publishing Platform,
North Charleston, SC.

Dedication

This book is dedicated to two extraordinary women, our grandmother and our sister Joyce. Everyone that came to our home called our grandmother "Mom." We think that was her name because people believed her to be a healer. Although we are thankful to many people who helped us along on our journey, Mom is the one that deserves this special dedication. We are sure that we would not have grown into the three women we are, if she had not been the woman she was then. My sisters and I hope the stories we heard about the early years will entertain you as much as they did us, and that the traditions Mom brought from Oak Island will benefit you and your family as much as it did ours.

On Valentine's Day 2016, Joyce joined Mom and other deceased loved ones, including her husband, Jim, who passed twenty years ago from Lou Gehrig's disease. Tiny Joyce cared for her husband as he slowly lost all ability to move and said it was her honor to serve him. He passed as Joyce held him in her arms. Joyce had the biggest heart of anyone in our family and truly loved all people unconditionally. She lived a life of acceptance and gratitude, even when we had next to nothing to appreciate, and our entire family stands in awe of her.

Our sweet sister Joyce found the silver lining in everything that came her way and in every person that walked through her door. She was the youngest sister and has beaten us through the door we all must enter, and we believe that we will see her again on the other side. The Mi'kmaq people, native to Nova Scotia, do not have a word for "good-bye" because it is too final, and they say nothing about life or death is ever final. Instead, when it is time to part for the day or for a lifetime, they say with confidence,

I WILL see you again.

Table of Contents

Prologue – A Rendezvous With Destiny

As some are aware, many of the related stories of the Money Pit have not yet been revealed to the public. Additionally, many of our family's barriers have been dissolved by the passage of time, leaving us with information to share. Every known piece of the puzzle brings us all a step closer to solving the elusive mystery. With so many people searching and researching, for so many years, someone is bound to stumble upon the missing answers eventually.

Currently the Lagina brothers lead the search, with the support of the Blankenship's, and new open lines of communication with Fred Nolan. I applaud their efforts to work together, because the clues seem to be hidden so well that it may take all of humanity collaborating to find the answer. The Lagina brothers began sharing their discoveries on 'The History Channel,' you may have seen the television series, **"The Curse of Oak Island."** If you caught the last two episodes in 2016, you are acquainted with the McGinnis sisters. Daniel McGinnis initiated their connection to the Money Pit Treasure search in 1795, and it has grown into a historical classic mystery. I am Kerrin, the daughter of Jean

McGinnis, and last year I accompanied my mother and aunts to be guests during the filming of the show. Although we brought stories of the past, I am excited about the technological advances being made, and the future that holds answers for the Oak Island mystery.

There have been many discoveries on Oak Island in the twenty-first century, but the veiled secret has consumed people for almost a quarter of a millennium. Oak Island is more than an interesting mystery whose suspense has continued for 221 years, it is a powerful magnetic source. Even though we have no way to reveal what the original artifacts were as seen by the discoverer's, we do know it was enough to compel three men, McGinnis, Smith and Vaughn, to dedicate their lives to the search. Although the exact words were not recorded, the actions of the next five generations of McGinnis men clearly indicates that they were driven if not obsessed. This obsession can serve as partial evidence, based on the fact that a family would not set their offspring up for failure to continue searching if there was nothing to find. Based on the dedication of my family I say that the pit was not a hoax created by the three founders and that the treasure remains hidden in its place, awaiting the next seeker.

The clues left behind continue serving as a strong enough force to propel the search for answers. I believe there is no need for supposition or speculation, because so many of the currently known facts of Oak Island are telling and extraordinary on their own. I consider Oak Island to be like a clawed hand, much like the man-made drain system in Smith's Cove, which resembles five fingers spread out over 145 feet of beach. I had this initial thought because I felt it grab ahold of me. I envision that hand latching deeply into some souls, while it lets others slip through its fingers. A very interesting fact is just how far-reaching that clawed hand extends around the world, and how those fingers hook into a variety of people from all walks of life from President Roosevelt to John Wayne to you and to me. When the treasure is unearthed, I hope one of the secrets that will be revealed is the common denominator that all these people share. What is it that gives Oak Island such a firm grip over us all?

As family narrator, I speak in the voices of the many members of my family who have revealed their stories to me over the years. I have verified some of the stories during my visit to Oak Island and others through extensive research. The rest are either too badly distorted to have credibility, or have not been previously recorded and only being shared for the first time in this writing. To remain in context with my family members as secondary sources, I will also give a brief insight into them as they tell their stories, which is realized to only be hearsay.

The purpose of this book is to call anyone with information forward. If we all share what little bits we think we know, it may help point out the right direction. Other clues to the mystery exist and remain “out there” unrevealed, simply not recognized for what they are or for the insight they can offer. A fresh perspective or a shared scrap of information may allow the many puzzle pieces to align in a new way, disclosing a clearer picture of the truth of Oak Island, and help the people in its’ grip to head in the right direction. Even a boundless journey begins by putting one foot in front of the other, or as a Chinese Philosopher said, “A journey of a thousand miles begins with a single step.” Let’s begin our journey together stepping in the right direction.

Chapter One:

Jean Begins The Untold Story

There is more than one island in the western hemisphere that has been named after oak trees. This book refers to an island off the coast of Nova Scotia where mysterious clues lead people to believe that something special is hidden beneath the land. Most books about Oak Island begin their first chapter with the exploits of a young Daniel McGinnis, but no book has told the story as our family passed it down. Our Grandpa Bill relayed our family history, with many stories he heard from his grandfather, which were told to him by his grandfather, who was Daniel McGinnis. The family story of the discovery of the money pit started differently than what is written, with the verbal rendition telling of Daniel living a full life before 1795. Daniel McGinnis sailed across the Atlantic, fought in the Revolutionary War, and got married in Nova Scotia before finding the money pit. Daniel was not a teenager in 1795, but a thirty-seven year old man.

Family Introductions:

Daniel McGinnis The stories I heard about our late - great - treasure - hunting - grandfather made me think he was the bravest man in the world, but you can read the stories and decide for yourself. Our family tree has four generations growing on Oak Island, and branches out from Daniel's second son, Daniel, to his son George, to his son George, to our Grandfather. George was a very popular name in the McGinnis family.

George William McGinnis : Our Grandpa Bill grew up on Oak Island and married our grandmother, **Rhoda Hiltz.** They had eight children: **George, Wally, Albert, Ambrose Lindsay, Roy, Mildred, Ida** and her twin **Charles,** who died at birth. Grandpa Bill had a gift for speaking, and his stories of Daniel painted a picture in my mind of life on the island over a century before.

Ambrose Lindsay McGinnis, my father married **Esther Elizabeth** in 1944, and had four children, of whom I am the oldest. They said I was named after my Uncle Wally's first love. Growing up, we did not have many things, like a television or radio, but the family stories of Oak Island were special and intriguing. I would be described as the believer.

The next oldest in our family is my sister Joan. Many noticed Joan on the 'The History Channel,' because she did most of the talking about receiving the gold cross from our brother Jim. As a nurse, Joan has the gift of compassion she extends to her patients and all those around her. Who knows what our family would have done without our practical Joan, especially when she served for years as our Brother Jim's caregiver.

Our youngest sister was Joyce, and she was the sweet one. Our precious Winnie Joyce was named after a child who would have been our aunt, but the child died years ago in a fire in Nova Scotia. Joyce questioned everything, even when she was young. She and I were polar-opposites in perfect balance, with the open-minded skeptic on one side and the unrelenting dreamer on the other side. Our skeptical Joyce is the reason for this book and our trip to Oak Island. She was the beginning of so many good things, and how this Oak Island adventure all began.

Our next sibling was James Edward Lindsay McGinnis; we called him Jim. The night he passed away, Joan was caring for him. He took the cross from his neck and put it around hers and said, "Do not let it out of your sight, and don't ever lose sight of the cross. It is the key."

Jim's insights into Oak Island are unique and more details can be found in his chapter, but we can let you know right now that the only concrete thing we can say about the cross is that it has been in our family as far back as we can remember. Our father wore the cross after Grandpa Bill, and our uncles seemed envious that Ambrose Lindsay received it. Our brother, Jim, wore it before he went to serve in the Vietnam War and wore it every day we saw him. Beyond those facts, the information is only what we heard.

Joan said, *Jim told me there were a few items that had been found while digging and they were put in three small boxes for the families of McGinnis, Vaughn and Smith. This is what I was referring to when saying there were three treasure chests. If a real treasure was found, I believe my family would have lived a different life, and they would have let future generations know so they would stop looking. My brother Jim was planning how he could get back to Oak Island until the day he died.*

Our uncles had items that they said came from Oak Island. We have asked our cousins, but they are not sure what happened to the gold nugget, and we have searched for more of our cousins to ask, but have not located them. We are hoping this book may bring some people forward that have other pieces of information, or actual artifacts, that have come from Oak Island, and that may possibly reveal another clue. If you have any memories to share, contact information can be found in the back of this book.

It may sound strange that we grew up unaware of the fact that Oak Island and the story of treasure was well known, but it was something talked about often at home and rarely in public. I don't remember my family telling me not to discuss the island, but I did notice that my uncles had their strategic meetings when it was just family in the house. At one point, all of our uncles lived with us and that home was filled with discussions and plans of finding the treasure. As a child, I told friends about Oak Island, and they did not believe me, so I did not mention it often outside of my home. After I was married at nineteen and started to tell my children the stories I had heard about Oak Island, I was awakened to the realization that my husband thought it was nonsense as well.

Our revelation began when Joyce had a friend that visited Nova Scotia in the early '80's. While her friend was there she saw a book with Joyce's last name in the first chapter, so she brought back a copy of the book. Joyce saw the name Oak Island and could not believe the stories we heard were in a book, so she ordered copies for all of us. Joyce seemed surprised that the island even existed, because she was just a baby when we visited Oak Island and did not remember any of the trip. Even the "believers" were quite surprised to see our surname in a book. That was the moment we realized that maybe our family was not just full of crazy stories. The written words about Oak Island and Daniel McGinnis made us think that our family stories were almost right, but after researching we were surprised to find their verbal renditions to be accurate according to the Nova Scotia archives.

We have two more brothers, Marty and Joey, by our mother and stepfather. Our wonderful brother Joey died tragically at a young age. Our Mother struggled to keep our family of six children together, and deserves recognition for her sacrifice; she also died way too young. Joan says, *Our memories are dedicated to our mother, Esther Elizabeth McGinnis.* During a family vacation to Nova Scotia in 2009, our brave brother Marty blazed a trail to Oak Island for me. A later chapter describes how we snuck onto the island, but were caught as trespassers, and escorted off Oak Island.

I feel like my life was shaped in part by what came from Oak Island and also by what was never found. It's interesting, the residue a loved one's perspective can leave on your own personality. I can look back and see the path of tenacious choices that I made based on the stories I embraced, and how that weaved the guided path to where I now stand. I can also see, through my family history, a trace of the remnants left from searching for treasure and the void of not finding it.

In my heart of hearts, I believe the treasure will be found if we all work together. I hope it is found during my lifetime, because I think when the treasure is uncovered it will explain the power and draw that Oak Island has had over so many people …. including myself.

The McGinnis men were so very different, so they each have their own chapter, but they all have the commonality of been bitten by the Oak Island bug. Our father and uncles would sit around the kitchen table strategizing, drawing plans and studying maps. What I could hear of the discussions sounded like heated debates. I often heard them talk about going back and finding the treasure. To the best of my knowledge they never gave up the search.

They had some information they kept secret, and when I walked in the kitchen they would say, “Little pitchers have big ears.” I did not understand what they meant at the time. I felt badly that they would stop talking when I came in the room, because it sounded so exciting and I wanted to hear more. As I reminisce, I am realizing that my appetite for Oak Island has always been insatiable. I remember the draw Oak Island held for me at a very young age. It is one of my earliest memories … a longing to hear more and wanting to explore.

The following chapters will be a compilation of discussions we were lucky enough to hear, along with some stories from each uncle and our grandparents. The book was laid out by design for the Prologue and First Chapter to have briefly answered all the questions we saw posted after the appearance on,

"The Curse of Oak Island." We did this so people can read the information freely on Amazon, and only the people interested in our family stories will purchase the book. My sisters and I hope you enjoy reading the stories as much as we enjoyed hearing them.

Chapter Two:

Sitting On Grandpa Bill's Knee

Sitting on Grandpa Bill's knee was a wonderful experience, since he was an amazing storyteller. Everyone, young and old, would gather around when he started talking. His words would paint a picture in my mind about how hard life was a century ago on Oak Island. While we sat on his lap he would let us touch the cross on his neck, and I remember counting the different sized holes. Five holes in each arm, three for the head and two in the middle making the top half have a total of fifteen holes. There are ten holes in the long bottom piece of the cross, some of the holes are round and some are triangular. Grandpa Bill loved to tell stories about every part of Oak Island, and everything he knew about Daniel McGinnis.

Grandpa Bill came to visit us in the States but said he did not travel like Daniel McGinnis had. When there, he would tell stories about his great-great-grandfather; who started long ago on the Isle of Skye and ended on the Isle of Oaks. He frequently told us we came from good Scottish stock. He said

Nova Scotia translated means the New Scotland. He said his grandfather called it New Alba, and I looked that up to find it is a Gaelic phrase used to express allegiance to Scotland. Translated into English, New Alba means "Scotland forever," literally Scotland until judgment.

Grandpa Bill talked about the stars, and said Daniel knew much more about the empyreal realm than he did. It should not be a huge surprise that people living centuries ago were more in tune with nature, but interesting to see how many mundane daily tasks were scheduled according to the position of the celestial bodies. Grandpa Bill handed down information about fishing and planting gardens during certain phases of the moon. Living in the 21st century, I think most people have turned their back on the guidance of the constellations.

Grandpa said that Daniel was a jack-of-all-trades. He hunted and worked the land as a true yeoman, and he fished and worked the sea as a true sailor. He began a seafaring life when he was a young boy growing up on an island in Scotland. Grandpa Bill would try and use a Scottish accent when he quoted old Scottish sayings from Daniel. I forgot most of them but this one is easy to remember, "Auld Lang Syne," which means long ago. I think of my grandfather when I sing the Scottish words at midnight every New Year's Eve. He started many stories with the following words that I heard so many times that I think I have them close, if not verbatim.

Over a century ago, when there were towering Oak trees on the east end as thick as ten men around, Daniel arrived on the Isle of Oaks. The strange Oak trees rose majestically above a sea of evergreens and the discoverers of the pit walked the island auld lang syne. Daniel and Mary were resourceful settlers and carved out a nice life for their family on the Isle of Oaks in New Alba. It was hard work, mind you, but none of your grandparents ever shied away from manual labor. The only way to be proud of your work is to work hard at it. Grandpa Bill would continue on at this point and tell of a successful McGinnis moment, or say a recent achievement someone in the family made.

One story was never enough, and we often asked Grandpa if he had time for a second. He'd laugh and say, "time does not matter because it is noon somewhere in the world." When I was old enough for happy hour and started to hear the saying, 'It's five o'clock somewhere,' I would think of my grandfather and wonder if someone copied his idea.

I could tell that Grandpa Bill was very impressed and influenced with the life Daniel led. He seemed to revere our progenitor, and he would say if he were a younger man he would be a sailor like Daniel was. It is impressive to sail across the Atlantic, especially in the 18th century. After making that journey as a teenager, Daniel sailed along the North and South Carolina shore and as far south as Florida. Grandpa loved to tell sailing stories that he heard and I can remember parts of a few, but not enough of the story to retell it.

The one sailing story I do recall clearly was about Daniel sailing in Scotland. My grandfather said that is where the sailing skills of our family began. Daniel taught his children so they could teach their children and so on down the line. While he was sailing in the Irish Sea, Daniel would say that deteriorating weather was something to look out for, but even more treacherous than ominous black clouds on the horizon is spotting a boat flying the Isle of Man flag. You must make sure and steer clear of anyone flying the three-legged flag.

I don't know much about either island in Scotland, but I would love to explore both of them. According to Daniel, the Isle of Skye was colorful with hidden pixie homes and the Isle of Man was grey with moors full of trolls. Recently, while I was boating with my daughter, we came across a sailboat with the flag of the three legs running and I told my grandchildren the story that Grandpa Bill passed down. Grandpa would grab my leg when he said, "They have three legs on their flag, because Isle of Man was known for chopping off a leg so that men could not escape." He would give my leg a squeeze and say, "when you see a boat flying a flag with three legs – jibe the other way and start running, while you still can run." The children onboard had a bunch of questions, so they looked it up on their phones, but did not find the Isle of Man story.

Grandpa Bill had many stories, but the story I remember the best is the discovery of the pit on Oak Island. All the grown-ups in my life told that story, but the way Grandpa Bill told it was my favorite. According to him, it was a woman who was the first to notice the special area that became known as 'the money pit.'

My grandfather said that Mary, my great-great-great-great-grandmother, was the person to discover the mark someone left in the area. Grandpa Bill said, "Once upon a time, on the Isle of Oaks, there lived a handsome man with strawberry blond hair and green eyes," he would pause to smile at me, "just like yours Jeanie. His wife had auburn hair and deep, dark eyes like Joan's. Mary was a quiet girl and just like you Joyce, she was very observant. One lovely afternoon the young, married couple chased each other in the woods. Daniel caught Mary and lifted her high and swung her around till they were dizzy and both fell to the ground laughing."

Grandpa asked us, "Have you ever laid down on the grass and looked up at the sunlight sparkling through the leaves?" We all said, "No, let's go."

Grandpa Bill had the most wonderful belly laugh that shook his whole body down to the knee I was sitting on. He said, "It's a little cold outside, so let's just use our imagination till spring. Just close your eyes and try to see the sparkles. Imagine that the leaves are such a bright green that they almost hurt your eyes to look at." I remember him explaining that the circles of light look like they are dancing on the leaves, when it's really the leaves that are moving in the gentle breeze.

He said, this is what your Great-Great-Great-Great-Grandma was squinting to see when an unnatural shape caught her eye. She said she thought she was seeing things, but the arrow was still there even after she squinted a little harder. It looked odd how the line pointed straight down while following the natural curve of the bark. She was drawn closer and Daniel asked Mary where she was going, but she did not say a word and just walked as if in a trance to the tree. Mary later said she thought if she looked away that the line would vanish into the tree and she would never find it again. Daniel followed her to the spot where she touched the mark. All Daniel saw was a carved and blackened mark on the side of the bark and asked, "What is that?"

Mary said, "That is not what it looked like," and she held his hand so that they walked backwards a few feet. Never taking her eyes off of the mark she guided her husband to lie down next to her; from this perspective the arrow was there before them and Daniel said, "Keep the heid." Grandpa explained that, translated from Scottish that means to stay calm.

Grandpa Bill said many families lived on the Isle of Oaks for many years, maybe this subtle yet powerful message is the reason the pit was not discovered earlier and part of the motivation for McGinnis, Smith and Vaughn to dig. Grandpa asked, "Do you know what Daniel told his sons, John, Daniel and Henry when he told them this story?" He told them that he was afraid at that moment. He had been a prisoner of war and felt the hairs on his neck raise when he was captured at gunpoint many years before, and he said he felt the same feeling as he lay in front of this arrow. This made him want to leave the area right away, but he faced his fear. Maybe the same magnetic pull that has drawn so many in, began at that moment with Daniel McGinnis. As he felt the deep connection and was compelled to return to the money pit, and talked friends into going with him, they began the search and I painted what I imagine the beginning to be like.

Daniel, John and Anthony painted by Jean McGinnis

When he told this story Daniel would look into his sons' eyes with his penetrating green stare and tell them, "You will feel afraid at different times in life, and that is okay. You can feel fear, but then you have to conquer it." The moral of the story continued on to explain that it is best to face fear head on and fast, so as to not think too long or the fear could immobilize you. This is a lesson that was passed down from each generation along with a powerful story that Uncle Wally will share about young John McGinnis.

Chapter Three:

Childhood visit to Oak Island around 1950

The first time I remember meeting our grandfather Bill, I was about five years old. The entire family met in Nova Scotia, Joan was four, Joyce and Jim were babies. I am sharing what little I do know about it, because I find it very suspicious that we took that trip.

This is the view from the McGinnis cabin, all that is left now is the stone foundation.

Our grandfather, George William McGinnis, was there, and I remember everyone showing him a lot of respect. The children called him Grandpa Bill. Our grandmother, who everyone called Mom, was there caring for all of us. I vaguely remember meeting my Great-Grandmother, Bessie McGinnis, and I think the memory comes from hearing my uncles talk about our trip and 'Ole Bessie.

We spent a lot of time outside in the cold. We walked through the woods and Grandpa Bill pointed out different paths that Daniel had made, and had names for them. We walked along the shoreline to Smith's Cove and he said when he was young there was a perfectly straight line of fifteen Oak trees along the point. There were no evergreens along the line, only large Oaks. The clearest memory from the walks is the story of Daniel fighting bravely in the war, and that he now guards the woods of Oak Island as a courageous soldier. I think this memory is so vivid because I was terrified of a soldier ghost at the time, but now I would love to meet him.

Grandpa Bill told how Daniel helped win the battle for the loyalists in the year 1780. I later looked up the facts to see if I remembered it right, and the largest surrender of American troops of the war, was at the battle and Siege of Charleston, South Carolina. I understand why my grandfather made such a big deal about it, because it could have turned the coarse of history. Daniel was a gunboat captain during that important battle that gave the British control of the waterways and all the southern colonies for a brief period of time.

I know this is not a lot of new information to be able to share, but I'd like to point out that the entire family coming together for this trip is interesting because of how poor we were. I have to wonder about what would make my entire family spend money on traveling to Canada? The train ride was such a big deal; I remember sleeping on the train and what a thrill traveling was, and still is for me. I can't say with certainty what happened in 1950 in Nova Scotia, but I believe it was something of substance.

I have a few crystal clear memories from that family visit and one is that it was cold, so I guess that doesn't narrow down the travel dates because it can be cold on the coastline of Nova Scotia anytime of year. A silly memory that stands out is going in the woods with my Mother to use the bathroom. We were close enough to see the ocean even in the pitch-black night.

The night sky I remember like a dream, because the stars were so bright that it looked surreal in my memory, until I returned as an adult to see them shine as brightly as I remembered. One night we made a very large fire under the moonlit sky and had something like a picnic in the dark by the fire. It was like a campfire, but bigger, as I said all things on Oak Island seem magnified. They threw a dead evergreen onto the fire and it exploded.

There was a very large fireplace in a tiny cabin and I remember the very small room crowded with grown-ups. I believe we slept next to the fire and the cooking was done outside in a large pot. The small home was overflowing, with all my uncles and their families in the tiny cabin. I do not think my father, Ambrose Lindsay, travelled with us, although he could have showed up for part of it, he was that elusive. I am not even sure of how long we stayed, but to a five-year-old, it felt like weeks.

I reconnected with my cousin, Barbara, and asked if she remembered the trip to Nova Scotia. She is a year younger than me but remembers the ride in the rowboat. My sister Joan said she remembers the sea being as calm as a lake and wanting to touch it. She said she tried to stand up in the boat, but our Mother made her sit down.

To say my family was not the ordinary American family taking a typical vacation would be an understatement. Maybe because most of my family is Canadian, there is never a dull moment when they all get together, and the memory is of a joyous time. I only remember one sad moment during that visit. One of my uncles had asked about their grandfather George and Grandpa Bill said, "When my younger brother Ambers drown a few weeks after his 18th birthday, my father turned his back on the island he loved."

Today I wish I could ask more questions, like where and how did he drown, but at the time I saw his deep grief and just wanted to change the subject. He had tears in his eyes when he said it was just before Christmas thirty years ago when he lost his brother. I am relieved that Bessie was not in the room to be reminded of losing her son. This story is validated and the death certificate is in my father's chapter, because he was named Ambrose Lindsay, after the uncle he never got a chance to meet.

Chapter Four

Second Trip To Oak Island

In 2009, my sister Joyce, brother Marty and I had brought some of our family to the hotel called The Atlantica, it is across the bay from Oak Island. We had hoped to be able to retrace our roots, but we were not allowed on Oak Island. It was still a thrill for all of us to see the plaque in the hotel lobby with the name Daniel McGinnis engraved on it. We were asking around for things for the kids to do and were told about a tour that went out on the night of the full moon to look for the ghost ship of the Young Teazer. My kids say that my face went white as I listened to the lady talk about the sightings of the ghost ship. My daughter Raina laughed and said I looked like I had seen a ghost. Nobody laughed after I finished telling the story as I heard it many years before.

We all went to the veranda of the hotel, and I told them the story of Daniel McGinnis and the ship called The Young Teazer. I told them a little about their great-grandfather Bill. He was an honorable man and many of his stories had a moral obligation. He was a soldier before becoming a fisherman, fishing the water around Oak Island like his father had. Grandpa Bill would begin the story saying that his grandfather, George, claimed to have become a farmer instead of a fisherman because of what happened to his grandfather, Daniel.

Daniel told his grandson that he was in his small boat the day the Young Teazer was blown up by one of its fearful crew. He claimed to have saved a badly burned man from the sea. Daniel also said that exactly one year later, he saw a ghost ship of the Young Teazer. This is the story as I heard it.

Daniel was a successful fisherman, and worked till sunset many days. As the sun dipped into the warm sea, he said he felt a chill travel through his entire body despite the balmy temperatures. He said all of a sudden he felt eyes upon him and instinctively looked to the ocean to see if a shark was watching him. It was in the broken reflection of the water's surface that he first saw the burning ship. He looked up to see the Young Teazer heading straight for him, and his small skiff. He could only think of two choices and knew he had to pick one and act on it fast, so he decided not to jump in the ocean and chose instead to stave off the oncoming ship with his oar and push himself to the port side of the burning hull.

His moral of the story, and philosophy on life, was to stand up and take action. I am guessing my great-grandfather George took a different lesson to heart and decided to never go boating at sunset. The lesson I learned from this story was to listen to my five senses. According to Daniel, he did not smell the billowing smoke or feel any heat from the flames as the burning ship approached. He was surprised as he reached out with the oar to see the entire ship vanish, and said he almost fell overboard attempting to stave off thin air. If I am sensing the exact opposite of what I am expecting to experience, then I think of this story and reevaluate my situation. If I am questioning what I am seeing and hearing, then I take a second look and listen again.

I thought these were wise words, but the look on my grandchildren's faces let me know that I was not the raconteur that Grandpa Bill was. I told them when I was little and my Grandfather told this story he would pretend to fall asleep at the most exciting parts of the story. Grandpa Bill would close his eyes and start to snore, so we all tickled and poked him till he got enough attention to finish his story. He startled himself awake and we all laughed. My grandkids laughed a little half-heartily, and I had the feeling that they would not wake me and would just pick up their phones if I pretended to fall asleep.

Joyce was famous for her one-liners and hugged me after the story whispering in my ear, "A ghost ship is as real as the story of Oak Island." That statement could be taken two ways; ghosts are not real and neither are any of the Oak Island theories or ghosts are real and so is Oak Island. I chose to believe the latter.

My family's extraordinary stories make the division of truth and fantasy anything but a straight line. To find out there really was a boat called the Young Teazer, that burned in Mahone Bay, I guess he could have seen a ghost ship 200 years ago in the year 1814.

After our trip to Nova Scotia, and seeing the Oak Island collection in the Atlantica hotel, I could understand what keeps driving this story on. It made me wonder what are all the facts that I had not yet heard. I asked at the hotel desk for more stories about The Young Teazer and was inspired to buy a book called, "Bluenose Ghosts," by Helen Creighton. The story she wrote of the Young Teazer was eerily similar to the one I had heard, and even reminded me of some parts of Grandpa Bill's story that I had forgotten, but the shocking part came in a different section of her book. She wrote about the soldier ghost visiting fellow treasure hunters on Oak Island. I made a concerted effort to not make assumptions when writing this book, but one cannot discuss ghosts without at least a little speculation. When I read the reports in her book of three different treasure hunters that claimed a soldier wearing a red coat walked up to them, spoke and told them they were digging in the wrong place, I wondered if they had heard Grandpa Bill's story of the soldier ghost or if the ghost is real.

What are the odds of someone seeing a man wearing the same uniform Daniel would have worn? While you are answering that question, consider the fact that the people who reported seeing a soldier in a red coat carrying a musket had no idea that Daniel had been a loyalist.

According to the majority of stories about Daniel, he would have been a baby during the Revolutionary War. Because it is beyond curious that they saw a ghost in a red coat, when I got to go back to Oak Island for the third time, I looked with an open-mind as I walked the woods, but did not get to meet my late-great-treasure-hunting grandfather that trip. I imagine that Daniel knows all the secrets of Oak Island now, and although his ghost has not pointed anyone in the right direction yet at least he stopped them from digging in the wrong place. I can imagine his Daniel's confident air, as he leans against a tree and nonchalantly says, "You are digging in the wrong spot mate."

The ghost of Daniel McGinnis

Painted by Jean McGinnis

Chapter Five

Uncle Wally had a Gold Nugget

As far back as we can remember, Uncle Wally wore a gold nugget around his neck. We've asked our cousins if they know where it is, but it has not been seen for decades. We had been told that this item came from Oak Island, but all that can be said for sure is that we remember him wearing this as a necklace.

Sometimes we would try to reach for Uncle Wally's gold nugget when he would tell us bedtime stories, but he would not let us touch it. Although this was 60-plus years ago when we listened to the following tale, it is one I don't think any of us will ever forget.

Uncle Wally began, "This is a story about young John McGinnis, Daniel's oldest son, and how his father planted a seed for heroism in him when he was very young." It really started when John was just 6 months old in 1798 and Daniel came back from a meeting on the mainland and announced that he heard about a young lad in Halifax that jumped into his small boat and helped save sailors that were on a sinking ship.

The news that evening was that the La Tribune went aground and over 300 men lost their lives. The waves were too rough for safety boats, but a young, 13-year-old orphan named Joe jumped in a skiff and rowed out to save a few men that were hanging onto the sinking ship. The action of this young teenager moved the adults that were immobilized by fear to help. Because of Joe, some of the sailors did not die that day. At this point the story goes that Daniel asked his wife if she would like to give John the nickname of Jo and hope he grows up as brave and strong as that young lad.

Rumor has it that John was nicknamed Jo that day, and the children were told often about the story of the teenager named Joe and how important it is to not let fear freeze you in your tracks. Before Jo turned ten years old he was put to a terrible test and proved to the world that fear would not immobilize him.

It was a hot day in Nova Scotia and the children of Oak Island were playing together on the beach. Jo's younger sister, Barb, had an adventurous spirit and on this day she pulled a log into the water and balanced on it as she drifted out farther than she should have. She fell off the precarious float, and she tried to get back on the log but began floundering and choking. Jo heard her and raced in the water.

The other children were on the beach screaming, but Jo took action without hesitation. Barb and Jo held each other, while the rest of the children stood on the shore in a helpless panic. The children said they saw a lot of splashing and then the water went dead calm. Uncle Wally said John must have felt afraid but he conquered his fear and helped his sister.

Family legend says this was the day that Jo lost his nickname, and was referred to as John for the rest of his life. They say he was named after 'John the Baptist,' and on this day he proved to also be brave like his namesake was in facing death. This is where Uncle Wally would end his story for the night, but Uncle Roy would tell us another version of John's story that you can read in his chapter.

Joan said that Uncle Wally was her idol. *Gorgeously handsome, intelligent, talented, worldly-wise, good husband, wonderful father, and an excellent provider were the character traits of Uncle Wally. He was always so busy at work, yet he made the time to visit us regularly. He was concerned with our welfare and helped all he could. I spent time in his home and came to love and adore his wife, Aunt Marie.*

After we were grown, Uncle Wally and Uncle George made it back to Oak Island to do some treasure hunting. The brothers travelled together with Uncle Wally as the skeptic and Uncle George as an enthusiastic believer. Similar to the Lagina brothers, with Rick being like our Uncle George and Marty Lagina questioning each discovery like Uncle Wally. Wally lived his life as a skeptic, but this skeptic making the investment in a trip to Oak Island to dig for himself, makes it all the more intriguing to me.

Oak Island has drawn brother dig teams, also father and son teams. This made me curious about why Daniel did not turn to a brother, but instead talked two friends into digging by his side. My curiosity was so aroused that I ordered the birth records for McGinnis to see if Daniel had any brothers. What I found from my cousin Kel Hancock in Nova Scotia was that Daniel was actually Donald. Donald fought in the War on the British side and lost all he had in North Carolina. Many loyalist soldiers settled in Nova Scotia after the war, and this is where he got married and had children. To uncover Oak Island facts, you almost have to be a detective. Kel does some good Oak Island sleuthing for the oakislandcompendium.ca, where his group posts related stories of the search. The group does extensive research in an attempt to reveal to the public points of interest that may need further exploration, and their service is appreciated.

As I attempted some research, I was surprised by all the different spellings of the family name McGinnis, McInnes, McInnis, MacInnes and MaccKenis. Looking up the original name MaccKenis I found that it could mean from the clan of Kenis in Scotland. To answer the question of different spellings, when you look at the cursive handwriting that birth, christening, death and marriage licenses were recorded in, it is easy to perpetuate misspellings. The name Donald does look similar to the name Daniel, when written in the elaborate long hand of the time. An interesting fact is that he did not name any offspring Donald, but did name his second son Daniel. That fact leads me to believe that it was not a cursive misreading, but that Donald had changed his name to Daniel before his children were born. The name Donald is Gaelic and the name Daniel is biblical, but I am trying to refrain from blind speculation in this book.

I have heard people talk of Oak Island and question what motivated Daniel/Donald and his friends to keep digging past layers of logs, without having any clue about the complex tunnel and flood system that lay below. I think I would be driven to dig by an arrow and a nicely laid floor of flagstone for a year or two, but they invested their lives into the pit. I believe that much of the motivation comes from within. Oak Island acts like an area of magnetism to some and continually compels them to pursue the truth. People held in its grip almost have no choice but to keep searching, it is as if they are obsessed with finding out more.

Uncle Wally believed in a Curse that was placed on the McGinnis men. I heard different theories from my family about this curse, and each will be quoted in the chapter of who said it, but they all agree that it was placed by the Mi'kmaq people for something a McGinnis man had done. Uncle Wally's version was that Daniel was told not to dig a third tunnel, and that is why the curse was placed. Uncle Wally would tell his stories until the most exciting part, till all three of us were on the edge of our bed, and then he would make us wait till the following evening to find out what happened next. All you have to do is turn the page.

Chapter Six

Secretive Uncle George

Uncle George was the most influential man in my life. His stories had morals and helped us learn how to embrace the differences of each member of our family – as different as each was. I think all of the men in my life were in the military. My uncles and father may have been Freemasons, but I cannot say for sure. I never heard that discussed, except by Uncle George towards the end of his life.

As Uncle George aged, he developed a form of dementia and he shared a lot of information that I had never heard before. He claimed he and all his brothers knew of strange facts of Oak Island. He shared many stories at the end of his life, but I must make it clear that he was not in his right mind during the final years, so you can take this chapter with a grain of salt.

Joyce, George & Jean McGinnis

Towards the end of his life, Uncle George had no teeth left and he laughed at the oddest things. It made all the hairs on my arms raise when he would throw his head back and laugh out loud. Even though I was an adult at this stage, it was a little unnerving. He pointed a finger to my chest and said,

“Do you know how important your ancestors were? No, you don’t,” and with his gaping toothless grin he said, “but I am going to tell you.”

He claimed that Daniel’s father was sent from Scotland in 1773 to start Freemasonry chapters in America. Uncle George said that Daniel’s father moved his family to North Carolina. Uncle George believed that Oak Island was our family destiny. According to Uncle George, even though Daniel had this great purpose, it was said that Daniel lost some of his land on Oak Island in a Poker card game many years ago. I personally find this hard to believe because with all the childhood stories I heard; I have Daniel McGinnis as a hero in my mind. I am still enthralled with the many adventures of my great-great-great-great grandfather. I am considered “the believer,” and do not know what to think about Uncle George’s crazy stories, but I still remember him fondly.

Last year I walked into a restaurant called Corsairs, and a memory of my Uncle George flooded in. I had forgotten about many of his off-the-wall sayings, but this one came back to me when I posed under a large skull-and-crossbones sign that read “Corsairs.” Uncle George asked me many times, “Jeanie did you know that I am a brother to pirates and corsairs?” I would nod my head saying “yes Uncle George,” thinking to myself that many people in my family seemed like a group of pirates born a couple of centuries too late. If you ever find yourself waiting at the customs dock on Jost Van Dyke, stop in at Corsairs and tell them Uncle George sent you.

Again, I would like to qualify my statements. When I cared for Uncle George, he said things that I had never heard from him before, and at the end he did not remember his name. I have always been interested in anything to do with Oak Island, but this information came scattered amongst hysterical laughing and other stories. He said, "I told my son, but I am going to tell you too Jeanie, there is a secret hatch near the cabin. Send your sons to find the hatch and find what is inside. Warn them not to get lost in there." He did not explain where to find it, but said the entrance was just a few inches beneath the surface. The following story I remember well because he was so descriptive. Uncle George said there is a very bright blue circular salt pond, due east of the money pit. It will stand out to you as the bluest thing around, because not the sky or the sea is as blue as this pool. It is so blue that you cannot see the bottom, but south of this pool you can see the way to stop the floodwaters from entering.

I am attaching a piece of paper that Uncle George showed me. One time he pointed to the page and said this is just one piece of the puzzle, and it was kept hidden behind a stone in the wall of Daniel's cabin. He said the more you discover on Oak Island, the more you will need to find the rest of the pieces of paper. I do not know where the inscription was copied from and have no idea what the symbols mean. I am sure you are wondering why I did not ask him any questions, and the answer is sad, but the truth is that at the time I thought he was crazy.

My Grandpa Bill had a saying he would use when my sisters and I were talking nonsense: "Yur bum's oot the windae." He would use his fake Scottish accent and say, "this is what your Grandpa Daniel would have to say to that." That Scottish phrase is what I thought of when Uncle George showed me this paper.

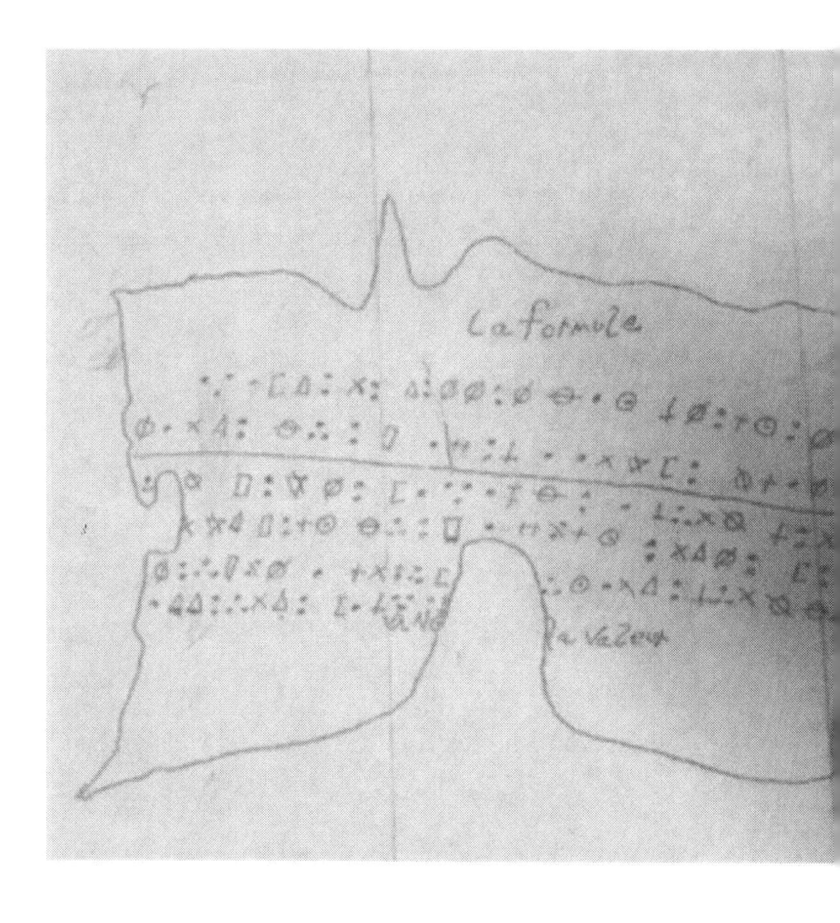

This is a copy of the one Jim had in his personal belongings that Joan kept safe. Jim's copy has notes in French that were written on the bottom of the page.

I feel our family barrier has come down in part due to the fact that I am no longer concerned with the stories I heard sounding outlandish. Long ago I married into a nice Italian family and desperately wanted my family to appear 'normal' to them. It was like trying to fit a square peg in a round hole, but today I am proud of the uniqueness of my family and I am proud to continue the quest for the secrets of Oak Island. The last stronghold was the men in our family, who liked to hide things in stonewalls and kept maps shrouded in secrecy. They have all passed, and the women want to get to the bottom of this. The McGinnis men all believed they were cursed, and if you look how each of their lives ended you may believe they were cursed. The curse does not seem to apply to the McGinnis women, so we may be free to explore.

I have no idea if anything Uncle George claimed was true, but maybe someone reading this can shed one more sliver of light on the subject. If anyone heard a family story of his or her great-great-great-grandfather winning a plot of land on Oak Island in a card game, please share your story. Towards the end of his life Uncle George announced that he had just sold his land on Oak Island for one dollar. Did anyone in the 1970's buy a piece of land on Oak Island for one dollar? The stories he told during the final years could be insightful to someone, or they could simply be the ramblings of an elderly gentleman.

Uncle George was an important man in our lives, and I don't want to remember just the later years even though they were quite colorful. He would spend a lot of time with us as children. He told stories and spoke of how hard it was to grow up being poor in Nova Scotia. His stories would make us feel better about how much we had – even though it was not much. Uncle George had high expectations and taught us many valuable lessons.

Joan said, *Uncle George, also my hero. Integrity always intact. He tried to teach me not to ever lie. That didn't take on me. I had to learn that one the hard way by making my own mistakes. He used to say, "Never lie to someone who trusts you and never trust any one who lies to you." Uncle George never lied.*

Uncle George was quite proud of me. I learned to read when I was three, and he was always there to help me with reading and spelling. He gave me money for spelling words correctly, $.25 for easy words and $.50 for the hard ones. He also taught me what it is to be frugal and save money. He taught me to drive and he was very strict and demanding. He spent a whole year just teaching me to park!

Uncle George did all the grown-up things that so many other adults in our life avoided. He sent money every month to his cousin Minerva in Nova Scotia to cover the costs of his sister, Mildred, who was born severely mentally challenged. When he lived with us, he was the one that tucked us in and told us our bedtime story. One of our favorites was Little Red Riding Hood, but naturally with an Oak Island twist.

The grandmother's house was on the Isle of Oaks, and Little Red Riding Hood was not supposed to go to the mainland. Uncle George would take this time to point out how important it is to listen and obey our Grandmother and Uncles. Little Red Riding Hood rowed herself across to Nova Scotia, and met a wolf on the mainland, and that mean old wolf tried to get Little Red Riding Hood to come with him. She was smarter than that and left the wolf, because no intelligent girl would walk off with a wolf. That big bad wolf found an old skiff and rowed across to Oak Island before the girl could return. The wolf attacked the grandmother, and locked her in the meat cellar but not before getting information out of her.

The big, bad wolf impersonated the grandmother. Funny how the senses can see, hear and taste what it is the mind expects. They were just ordinary fairytales with an Oak Island twist; some things like "The better to see you with my dear," stayed the same. You can probably guess the rest of Uncle George's story;

Little Red Riding Hood was resourceful in the original fairytale and in this version also. She let the wolf chase her through the woods and she jumped over the pit and the wolf fell to his grave.

Chapter Seven

Uncle Albert – Are you out there?

Uncle Albert was not consumed by Oak Island to the same degree that my other uncles seemed preoccupied with it. He was the only one that seemed almost untouched by it. He told stories, but he told them as if he were a student trying to absorb the facts, and some nights he sounded like a teacher telling a lesson at school.

What was obvious with my other uncles, was hidden with Uncle Albert. He always seemed a little "out there." When my uncles told us stories, they seemed to passionately believe what they were saying to have happened; even my Uncle Roy who spoke of fairies, spoke as if none of this were embellished. My Uncle Albert had a flare, and his stories seemed to be just that, a bedtime story, and at the same time, each of his stories would contain factual bits that would come in handy.

Uncle Albert would say, "If your life is hard and rewards are few, remember that the mighty oak tree was once a nut like you!"

He said he knew how Oak Island got its name and who planted the first Oak tree on the island. He would tell amazing stories of sailing across the Atlantic. He spoke of the sea and the men who explored it with a mixture of admiration and jealousy. Those brave men would say good-bye to their families and set out to sea, not sure if they would ever get to see them again.

On one of these journeys, the captain sailed from Europe to the Caribbean; the men got off the boat and collected coconuts. They traveled north to Florida and collected oranges. The next stop was Georgia, where they picked peaches, and he would tell the story going all the way up the East Coast. He is where my love of geography began. Uncle Albert said that there was a connection between where we lived in New Haven, Connecticut and Oak Island, Nova Scotia. The ship travelling up the East Coast stopped in the New Haven harbor in Connecticut and one of the sailors took a fancy to a squirrel and brought him on board as a pet. All the men fed the squirrel so much food that the squirrel never ate the nuts he carried in his mouth on the boat.

The boat travelled north and stopped at Oak Island, which was then called Gloucester Island, and called Smith Island by the locals. The squirrel went exploring on the island and was sad to find no food for himself, only pinecones. The next day, the squirrel brought a few of his stored nuts along for the day's exploration, and the sailors also brought some food for their day of exploring. The men shared with the squirrel, and the squirrel realized he liked people food better than nuts, so he left his acorns in the dirt and they grew into trees on Oak Island.

Joyce remembered Uncle Albert saying that, *Connecticut was a Nova Scotia word that the Mi'kmaq people used to mean "long river." He shared all sorts of interesting facts about the Connecticut River, and how it flowed. He loved to talk about all bodies of water, but especially the ocean.*

Joyce reminded me of a story that Uncle Albert would tell that got her in trouble in Sunday school. Joyce's faith in God was impressively strong, but she never let that faith limit her mind to think God had to be a man in a white robe. Joyce's faith was limitless like the ocean thinking of God as being everywhere for everyone. She told me once that she thought of herself as a small cork bobbing on the vast sea and the ocean was God's love for her. It was everywhere, it was so much larger than she could comprehend and yet it always kept the tiny cork lifted up. She lived her life afloat on a sea of God's light.

Uncle Albert's creation story started with the earth being one giant sea. Earth had no land and could only be inhabited by creatures that could live in the ocean. Ships from other planets would visit and float around the liquid earth for a while and then leave in search of land. On one of these trips, the spaceship accidentally left a girl behind. The girl was out swimming and called out, but the only thing that heard her was a large sea turtle.

The turtle called to his friends and they held on to each other and made a turtle island for the girl. Sea creatures dove to the ocean floor and collected sand for her and shells for her to collect rainwater. She managed to survive until a ship from another planet landed. The new spaceship was more advanced then her people, and they had a machine that looked like a big straw that pumped seawater out of the ocean and up out of the atmosphere. After six days and nights of pumping, land started to appear and on the seventh day everyone swam. They all settled on what is now known as Mount Ararat in Turkey. The turtles had faithfully served and were free to go and the girl named the new land, saying that turtles are the key, as in Turkey.

Chapter Eight

Uncle Roy was like an older brother to us

Uncle Roy was my grandparent's youngest son and fifteen years old when Mom and he moved in with us, so Roy was more like a brother to us. Uncle Roy would not only tell us stories, he would play with us too. We would go on fairy hunting adventures and search for fairies carpet (moss). He said Oak Island was full of fairies carpet.

Fairies are not discussed much today, but centuries ago it sounds like it was a natural topic of conversation in Scotland. You are reading a book and contemplating believing that people came across the ocean before the 17th century and built an elaborate system beneath Oak Island to house something; it is not much of a stretch to also believe that some fairies came along for the ride.

Uncle Roy would say if you ever see something strange unlike anything you have ever seen, it is okay to feel afraid but then you must acknowledge it. He guessed that fairies have shown themselves to many people at different times, but because they look strange and different, the people choose not to see. All of my uncles seemed so accepting of others, even during the 1950s, which was a conservative time in history. Some of my friend's parents did not allow their children to play with others that were not from the same church or the same ethnicity. Our home was open to all people, it seemed that the more of an outcast a person was, the more welcoming the McGinnis home would be to them..

Uncle Roy said that his father told the story of fairies that his grandfather, George, heard right from his Uncle John (Daniels oldest son). John told the story that he would never forget the experience of flying, and that he thought of death as a marvelous adventure. When John was a young boy trying to save his sister Barb, he said he remembers them both sinking to the bottom of the ocean together and then floating to the clouds in the sky.

He said that fairy lights flew with them, and they called him to come back.
The tiny lights helped him to look down. He said he was so happy flying with them that he did not really want to go back to the beach. He said it was a strange feeling watching his Dad push on him, but he was not in there, he was right here

in the air. He said he wanted to fly with the fairies some more, but they would not let him. He was jealous that Barb got to keep flying, but he was also very happy for her.

John said that the fairies were all flying around him buzzing "hurry," it was all so beautiful that he did not want to hurry but they flew around him like a little whirlwind lighting his back to the beach. He would say that he knew they are so little and cannot push, but it was like they all joined together and their wind pushed him back into himself. John said that he thought he lived a different life than he would have if he did not feel how wonderful it feels to be free of the body and fly. He thought he had something important to do on this planet, but as he grew he could not see anything important that he had done. He said he had not found the treasure, so always felt that he did not live up to his purpose. He also said that maybe one of his children might find it. Family rumor says that is the reason he had so many children.

Tiny lights of Oak Island, painted by Jean McGinnis

Our uncles said that 'ole Bessie told this story for the last time during our visit to Oak Island in 1950. Uncle Roy said that his Grandma Bessie often told him the story about the children on Oak Island going off to play after they did their chores one day. Children back then got all their work done before they played. The three children played hide and seek on the beach and then made the game a little more challenging by hiding in the woods.

Bessie said how she was strangely interrupted while hanging the laundry. She heard her name, and she stopped and looked around. She did not see anyone and realized that she did not really hear her name; it was more like feeling it. She would say it is hard to describe, but it happened again. It was like she was calling herself in her thoughts, but she never called herself Bessie when she was thinking. She had thought she was imagining things from being in the hot sun so she went inside and started to busy herself in the small kitchen. She got a cup of water and she said this time it was a loud sound saying in a voice she had never heard, "Your children need you."

She said it was like the words reverberated throughout her entire body until she shook and dropped the tin cup on to the floor and ran out the door down to the beach. She screamed for George, as she raced to the beach. Standing on the empty beach she could feel the taste of panic rise in her throat when there were no children in sight.

She said a buzzing sound began around her that helped her fight the immobilizing fear and somehow filled her with a feeling of relief that there was still time. She swallowed that awful panic taste and felt empowered, but she just did not know where to go. She spun in a circle screaming out and felt the fear seizing hold of her again, and then she said she noticed lights sparkling in the woods. It was such a bright day on the beach that she could not be sure, in her hesitation she heard a fluttering near her head that sounded like bees buzzing the word hurry… hurry… hurry, and so she did.

She ran straight to the tiny lights in the woods, and they lit a path leading her to the swamp. She almost ran straight into the swamp herself, but heard all the little voices that each had said "hurry" come together in one loud sound that said "STOP!" The children were sunk to their chest and struggling. Uncle Roy said that 'Ole Bessie was strong. She took charge and told the children to be still, and they obeyed right away as she gathered branches and laid them out. She screamed for help, but she could not wait. She climbed a tree and grabbed a vine and cut it off with her teeth, and then she ripped her skirt off and reinforced the cloth with the vine, tied it around a tree and saved the children one by one.

Grandma Bessie said she fell to the ground with relief, and as she lay with one cheek in the mud she saw a tiny pixie fly into a hole in the ground. 'Ole Bessie was a strong woman that lived through a lot, so no one laughed when she said the pixies helped her save her children. Today, the existence of fairies seems to be entertained only by young girls, but I have known grown men that believe that fairies have come and helped when they were needed the most. I have not seen a fairy yet, but I still believe.

My sister Joan remembers Uncle Roy *as fun. He taught me how to skate and ride my bike and play jacks. He would pull me in my wagon up to the top of a hill. Then he would go down to the bottom of the hill and hold his arms out to me. I would push off and go flying down the hill.*

Chapter Nine

Aunt Ida

I remember Aunt Ida as always being a bit eccentric. She had a bird in a cage that she would bring with her to our home to visit. She had an intense way of looking at people when she spoke. She did not tell us stories of Oak Island, and she did not like to speak of it. Aunt Mildred had a severe handicap and spent her days in a home in Chester.

My only memory of Aunt Mildred was that Uncle George sent money to Nova Scotia to pay for her care. I have a lot of wonderful memories of Aunt Ida, but none about Oak Island. She filled me with travel facts and gave me a taste for wanderlust. She travelled quite a bit, but she never talked about wanting to travel to Oak Island.

My sister wrote the story about playing hooky with our Aunt Ida one day. Joan said, *One cold November morning in Connecticut, Aunt Ida came to visit as she often did. I was twelve years old, in seventh grade. Aunt Ida talked me into skipping school to go clamming with her. She loved clamming but this would be the last time she would ever go.*

I put on my boots and heavy coat and off we went to Gulf Beach in Milford. We took our pails and headed for the fertile clamming spot at the edge of the tide. We meandered down the Atlantic coast for I don't know how long. What I do know is that I had lost sight of the parking lot where we had parked and I happily noticed that my bucket was almost full. Suddenly I heard Aunt Ida's voice and it sounded funny, sort of high pitched and squeaky at the same time. She said, "Joani, come and help me! Pull me out!" I started to go to her and "something" stopped me. I knew then as truly as I know it now, if I had tried to pull her out we both would have disappeared into the quicksand.

In a second I summed up the situation. I looked around, looked at her, and I knew it was bad. Really bad! Behind me empty ocean. Right and left no houses, no cars, not a sound. That is when I heard it, the sound of hammering! That was the good news. The bad news was that Aunt Ida and the pool of quicksand was between the hammering and me. She was sinking and time was running out. In an instant I simultaneously remembered Moms' words, "pray with faith." I threw a prayer up to Heaven that went something like, "GOD I need you! I know you will help me," and I suddenly realized I was running over the quicksand only it was slow-motion running. With every step the quicksand sucked my foot and leg down almost to my knee and I pulled with a strength I never knew I had, got it out and took another "running" step. It must have been a comical site to GOD and my angel with me mock-running away and Aunt Ida calling after me, "Joani where are you going?"

I reached the beach and headed straight toward the blessed sound of hammering. It was a crew building a house. They called the fire department. They came and laid down planks on the quicksand out to where she was in up to her chest. I stood in the cold rain and watched as they pulled her out and walked her over the planks to safety.

While she was being checked, I found a log on the beach and sat down to pray and thank GOD, my angel, and Mom for helping me to save her. As I prayed, I gazed at the ocean and listened to the wonderful sound of the surf. My gaze finally fell on my legs and feet and I felt a warm, delicious thrill move through my whole body as I realized there was no trace of quicksand on my legs or boots. About that time a priest sat down beside me and tried to talk to me but I couldn't speak. I know now that I was in shock. What was between the quicksand and me? It could only be my angel. So that was my first miracle, asked for and granted, but not my last. The gift of faith that Mom gave me came to fruition that day. There have been so many swamps and deep, dark holes with no way out that I have dug for myself, and when all hope was gone I finally remembered to pray with faith. HE has never failed me.

No way can I speak of Aunt Ida and not mention Uncle Jack. Her husband, Jack Moses ranks among the favorite uncles. And then there's Barbara, my cousin, sister by choice, my friend, my closest ally. Barbara is Aunt Ida's only daughter. We are the same age and we were inseparable when we were kids. Barbara and I were out of touch for many years. We recently connected again, because of this book, and it was just like old times: The sharing, the knowing, the laughing, and the understanding.

Chapter Ten

Ambrose Lindsay McGinnis

Ambrose told the story that he was named after a boy that drowned on Oak Island. As I did research to make our family tree, I found in the Nova Scotia archives that an Ambers McInnis died by drowning at 18 years old in 1920. All the other death records I looked at were completely filled out, even for newborn babies, like George McInnis who died at one day old in 1911. George Albert died at 4 months old in 1914, and the death record was completely filled out saying that he died of a sickness that came on suddenly. Information on the death record was location, and both babies had lived on Oak Island with their father, who was Grandpa Bill's brother, Edward George McInnis. The name George continued to be popular with the McGinnis family, well into the 1900's.

Ambers McInnis' death certificate is attached, because it is oddly blank. The parents, George and Bessie McInnis, my great-grandparents, lived on Oak Island after they were married in 1893. The marriage records state that George

McInnis was from Oak Island and Bessie Rafuse was from Gold River.

FORM 5

PROVINCE OF NOVA SCOTIA

CERTIFICATE OF REGISTRATION OF DEATH

549

1 PLACE OF DEATH—
County of Lunenburg Municipality of Registered No.
City or Town Martins Point Street House No.
If in hospital or institution, give name
2 NAME OF DECEASED Ambers McInnis
Residence

MARGIN RESERVED FOR BINDING

PERSONAL AND STATISTICAL INFORMATION

3 SEX: Male
4 RACIAL ORIGIN: Canadian
5 Single, Married, Widowed or Divorced (Write the word): Single
6 BIRTHPLACE (Province or Country): Nova Scotia
7 DATE OF BIRTH (month, day and year)
8 AGE: Years 18, Months, Days 22. If less than one day, hrs. or min.
9 LAST OCCUPATION OF DECEASED
(a) (Trade or occupation or kind of work)
(b) (Kind of industry)
(c) From 19 (Date from which so employed)
10 FORMER OCCUPATION OF DECEASED
(a) (Trade or occupation or kind of work)
(b) (Kind of industry)
(c) From 19 (Date from which so employed)
11 LENGTH OF RESIDENCE (in years and months)
(a) At place of death
(b) In province
(c) In Canada (if an immigrant)

Parents
12 Name of father: George McInnis
13 Birthplace of father (Province or country): Nova Scotia
14 Maiden name of mother: Bessie McInnis
15 Birthplace of mother (Province or country): Nova Scotia

16 Informant's name
Address
17 Relationship to deceased
18 Place of burial, cremation or removal
Date of burial: Dec 6th 1920
19 Undertaker: Mr David Zwicker Mahone Bay (Name and address)

MEDICAL CERTIFICATE OF DEATH

20 Date of death: Dec 2nd 1920 (Month, day and year)
21 I HEREBY CERTIFY, that I attended deceased from 19 to 19 that I last saw h alive on 19 and that death occurred, on the date stated above, at m.
The CAUSE OF DEATH was as follows:
drowned
(duration) yrs. mos. dys.
CONTRIBUTORY (Secondary)
(duration) yrs. mos. dys.
22 Where was disease contracted if not at place of death?
Did an operation precede death? Date of
Was there an autopsy?
(Signed) M.D.
Address
Date

State the Disease causing Death, or in death from Violent Causes, state (1) Means and Nature of Injury, (2) whether Accidental, Suicidal or Homicidal.

23 Registrar's Record Number
24 Filed Nov 14th 1921 James Haughn [illegible] (Registrar)

SEC. 46—Vital Statistics Act makes it the duty of the Undertaker or person acting as Undertaker to obtain all the particulars required in the "Certificate of Registration of Death" and to fyle the same with the Division Registrar who shall issue the burial permit. (OVER)

Ambrose Lindsay married our Mother, Esther in 1944 and they had four children by 1949. The three McGinnis sisters were born in New Haven, Connecticut and our little brother, Jim, was born in Ohio.

Ambrose Lindsay McGinnis

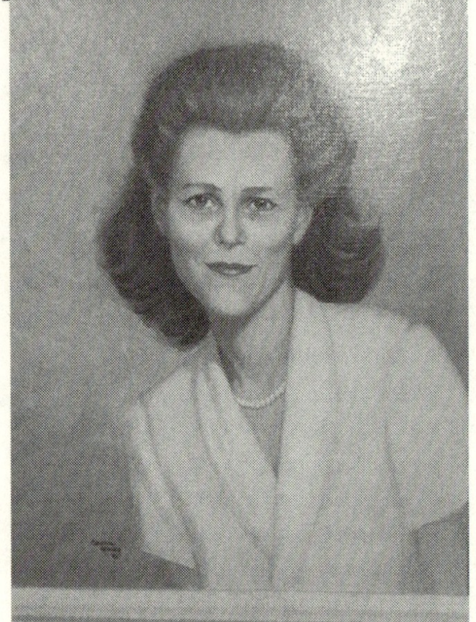

Esther Elizabeth McGinnis

I remember moving to Ohio and was told it was because my father was doing some secret work for the government, but what I remember the most is that just before Jim was born my father left for work one day and did not return. Our grandmother moved with her young son, Roy, and stayed with us in Ohio until Jim was born on the fourth of July. I remember seeing baby Jim for the first time. I watched Mom hand him a silver coin, which he held in his tiny fist as Mom proclaimed he would be prosperous. Jim dropped the coin and Mom shook her head looking down and said, but he will spend it foolishly. When Jim was big enough we all moved back to New Haven. I have fond memories of a home with a big apple tree in the backyard and all of our uncles lived there with us.

Mom was everything good in our life, we would kneel at her feet while she read from the Bible; she always made the stories so interesting. We never saw her drink or smoke or swear, and we never went to the doctor while she lived with us. She did not seem to judge and took care of everyone in need with the same loving hands.

Lindsay popped in and out of our lives throughout the years always with a grandiose story of one kind or another. He would tell us not to ask too many questions, because if we knew too much they would come after us. I still have no idea who 'they' were. He let us know during his life that he had to keep a lot of secrets. I thought when he passed some of the secrets would be revealed, but there was only an empty safety deposit box. He said his lawyer held the key, but we had to get a warrant to have the box cut into, only to find it empty. According to our father the law firm had pictures and sensitive documents, but have been unresponsive to our requests for the files. Looking back there were many unexplainable stories that surrounded Lindsay's life, and I am quite sure that I will never know the truth about most of them.

One of his many stories was that he could lead the way to the treasure by kicking over a single stone. He said he did not want to go to Oak Island because of the curse. He would tell us a story that there was a curse put on the McGinnis men because one of his uncles fell in love with a Mi'kmaq woman. He told so many stories, but I think the only true one was that he was as fond of women as my Uncle Albert was of the sea.

I share this information because I feel it is important to know that this man held very little as sacred, and yet held onto this cross and successfully delivered it to the next generation. He flitted in and out of our lives giving such small amounts of information, and I always thought his hints about secret missions was a lie; still, as an adult I would not be shocked if he turned out to have been a secret agent. If the cross is traced back to ancient times I will have to re-evaluate the man that I thought my father was.

Chapter Eleven

Brother Jim

This is a picture of a young James Edward Lindsay McGinnis. It is an old photo, but if you look closely you will be able to see he was wearing a cross.

It is impossible to tell if it is the same cross by the picture, but we remember him wearing the same distinct cross all of his adult life. The same cross with the holes in it that our grandfather wore. We know it is possible that Grandpa Bill could have acquired the cross somewhere other than Oak Island, but even when I realize this possibility there is still something that feels special about the cross. Joyce wore the cross when she was ill because she believed it gave her strength, and you may remember that she was skeptical of everything.

We cannot impress upon you in a single book how shocking it is to us that the cross survived Ambrose Lindsay and Jim's life. It is beyond surprising that it was not stolen, hocked or broken during their unconventional adventures. I cannot help but wonder if those two men were given more words that motivated them to succeed at keeping the cross safe. As we learned a little more of what our brother Jim lived through and gained more understanding into his life, just the fact that he kept the cross in sight is enough motivation for us to obey the words and do the same.

Anyone who knew Jim, would agree that "a unique character" is a good description of him and the life he led. I think his friend Phil summed Jim up the best. *Jim was always a bit spooky and enjoyed being unnecessarily secretive about a lot of things. He even used a call sign with his cell phone.*

Phil Bayly reflected on how his friendship with Jim began. *By chance, they were seated side by side in a restaurant following a Scientific Study Group meeting. From there, it did not take long until they were deeply engaged in conversation. Jim was a full bearded, very unusual-looking guy in his mid-fifties. He wore a small black sea captain's cap with a gold anchor in the front, gold chains around his neck and had a small parrot sitting on his shoulder.*

His eyes were dark, with an intense stare during conversation as if he were trying to hypnotize his subject. Phil thought, "Captain Ahab -- right there in the flesh!"

Tragically, he was also confined to a wheelchair to accommodate his very frail body that appeared to have seen much better days. Jim was a Vietnam Veteran, and he claimed to be a POW for a short while until he escaped to safety. However, his emaciated body was not the result of that heroic ordeal, but the result of his over-exposure to Agent Orange and its agonizing long-range effects.

Phil shared some enlightening war stories and intelligence work after the Vietnam War. This new information was astonishing, job descriptions about Jim being an assassin for the CIA, but not related to Oak Island so not included. I will let you know that Phil had stories about Jim that left me surprised to hear that Oak Island was interesting after their wild adventures. According to Phil, *The most intriguing subject we discussed was Jim's family legacy from the "Legend of The Money Pit" on Oak Island in Nova Scotia. It seems that Jim was a descendent of Daniel McGinnis, the original discoverer of the Money Pit on the Island. Jim proudly wore a heavy gold chain around his neck. He claimed it was handed down from his family as a stray remnant of the larger treasure never recovered. Jim's great-great-great-great-grandfather was with the Onslow Mining Company during its early efforts to recover the treasure. It and many other mining companies and other adventurers over the years, including President Roosevelt, had all unsuccessfully tried their luck recovering this purported huge treasure that is so cloaked in mystery. Numerous TV documentaries and books have been released over the years that revealed most of the basics, as well as details, of Jim's story as true.*

Of course, it was also Jim's dream to recover the treasure if there was any possible way. Jim felt advantaged from his family's linkage and inside secrets associated with its burial location, unusual conditions and other pertinent information needed for its possible recovery. To try to help Jim's dream come closer to reality, we did some additional research and enjoyed the work, having been bitten by the Oak Island bug. Strategizing about Oak Island kept Jim's spirits high in expectation, especially since he had so little else to look forward to with his failing health. Jim called Phil "his partner," and they actually had a serious recovery plan formulated.

They had maps and photos of the area as well as other data. They knew the boundaries and terms and conditions of everyone holding current Treasure Trove licenses for the Island and surrounding area. The information had primarily come through contact with the Nova Scotia Natural Resources Registrar of Mineral and Petroleum Titles Department, the local Chamber of Commerce and the local Historical Society for all of the official information available. They sent a copy of the painted symbols, along with a note they translated into French to be respectful of the recipients, and found everyone to be very responsive and helpful to their inquiry. They had even acquired some unique technically gathered data to throw into the growing database for improved correlation. This data came through a noteworthy treasure hunter friend, Tampa legend Gene Holloway, and his semi-secret molecular frequency discriminator equipment. That really lit the fire, since it provided a much higher probability of success for their project. Their initial game had more recently transitioned into a truly serious endeavor. Their plan was nearing completion even though they critically needed an investor.

Jim passed away before he could get back to Oak Island. When the discovery of Nolan's Cross was announced Jim called both Joan and I, saying he had to get from Florida to Oak Island. Jim's obsession proves to me that if the treasure has been found, it was not unearthed by a McGinnis – at least… not yet. The letter below is evidence of what Jim was working on during the final years of his life. We would like to acknowledge Phil for sharing so much of his time with our family, his wise words, and for keeping up with Jim's letter.

In reply to: Your letter, dated May 16, 2000

Nova Scotia Natural Resources
PO Box 698
Halifax, Nova Scotia B3J2T9

Attention: R.Ratcliffe

Subject: Oak Island Treasure

Dear Mr. Ratcliffe

This letter is to express my sincere appreciation for your timely and informative response to my initial letter of inquiry concerning my interest in the Oak Island Treasure. I found your letter and its attachments to be specific to my request and it provided additional pertinent information that was also of great benefit and insight to me.

In review of the data within the attachments to your letter, I found Schedules D – Special Conditions from the Nova Scotia Education and Culture Department to two of the Treasure Trove licensees (Mr. Nolan & Mr. Harvey). In the first paragraph of these memoranda, I further found reference to an "attached map" that identifies two small areas of unique interest for possible archaeological remains and the Department's directive protections accordingly. Unfortunately, those cited attachments were not included in the package you previously forwarded with your letter. Therefore, if they are available and releasable, I request you forward copies of them to me for my continued planning and considered courses of action regarding the recovery of the treasure. Within each of the Treasure Trove licenses, I also found omitted: Schedule C- the Work Program. I realize the licensees could consider this information proprietary and therefore not releasable; however, if not, I respectfully request copies of them also.

I recognize you and your office staff cannot continue catering to the detailed whims of interest and inquiries from the massive public and its interest in this historical treasure without reasonable compensation for your administrative efforts. Therefore, I have enclosed a modest personal check intended to cover the administrative costs associated with my prior and current inquiry requests. If the enclosed amount is insufficient, please advise me and I will forward the balance immediately.

Again, I sincerely thank you for your highly professional attention on this matter. As my plans continue, I will keep you advised.

Respectfully,

Mr. James E, McGinnis

19 June 2000

Nova Scotia Museum
1747Summer Sreet
Halifax, Nova Scotia B3H3A6

Attention: The Curator of Special Places, Mr Robert Ogilvie

Subject: Oak Island Treasure Trove Licences

Dear MrOgilvie

I am James E. McGinnis; a direct descendant of Dan McGinnis (McInnis) associated with the original history of the Oak Island Treasure. I have recently been in correspondence with Mr. Ratcliffe of your Government's Registrar of Mineral and Petroleum Titles Department concerning my interest in recovery of the treasure. See attachment A. In response to my initial inquiry, Mr. Ratcliffe provided me copies of the current Treasure Trove Licenses for Oak Island and nearby islands, including attachments. See attachment B. In two of those licenses' attachments, those extended to Mr. Nolan and Mr. Harvey, were also cited "attached maps". See attachments C & D. Within those attached maps are presumed cited unique locations within Mr. Nolan and Mr. Harvey's respective licensed areas that your Department has set aside as sanctuary unless further permission is requested and granted for activity.

In response to my subsequent inquiry to Mr. Ratcliffe for the attached maps, or the additional details therein describing location, he has referred me to you as the source of that information for request. See attachment E. Accordingly, I in turn now request and will be greatly appreciative if you will provide me with the cited maps or the information that describes the locations of the sanctuary areas. I need the information in whatever detailed manner your Department may have for my continued planning.

Additionally, I fully understand, appreciate and respect your Department's historical interest in Oak Island. Therefore, I extend to you and your staff an offer of full co-operation on my part to assist in any way possible, including contacts throughout my family, to recover any specific missing links of history that may be of benefit. This information may come from our best memory or documentation that is available. I openly invite you or staff at any future date to simply ask for any specifics in which I may be of help.

I thank you in advance for whatever assistance you may give to my requested information.

Sincerely,

James E. McGinnis

Attachments:
A: J. McGinnis letter dated April 28, 2000 to Nova Scotia Dept. of Natural Resources (Mr Ratcliffe)
B: Nova Scotia Dept. of Natural Resources letter dated May 16, 2000 (Mr. Ratcliffe to Mr. McGinnis))
C: Nova Scotia Dept. of Education and Culture letter dated June 16,1998 (Mr. Ogilvie to Mr. Nolan)
D. Nova Scotia Dept. of Education and Culture letter dated June 16, 1998 (Mr. Ogilvie to Mr. Harvey)
E. Nova Scotia Dept. of Natural Resources letter dated June 8, 2000 (Mr. Ratcliffe to Mr. Mcginnis)

We are searching for more of the documents Jim refers to, and will post as new information becomes available. When Jim was alive I was not convinced that he had so much information, but I am now and we will continue to look for it. You may have heard the story that on Jim's final night on January 30, 2006, he gave Joan the cross, and instructed her to never let it out of her sight and to never lose sight of the cross. Jim also told her he was instructed to pass information to Joan's son Danny. Jim had moved from Florida to be in California with Joan, but Danny was in Connecticut, so some valuable information may have been buried with Jim all because of gender prejudice. I think it would be fitting for a female McGinnis to discover the entrance to the tunnel system.

A year after Jim passed, Joan said she was approached in a store and asked why she was wearing a mason's ring. She was taken by surprise and honestly did not know she was doing anything wrong. She explained that her brother had passed and she liked wearing some of his things. The unknown gentleman said to her that other people would come to her home and take it from her. From that day forward she only wore Jim's cross necklace and left Jim's ring in a safety deposit box.

The family remembers Jim as secretive, resembling Ambrose Lindsay in some ways. Jim never explained any of his behavior to us when he was alive, like why he would stop by for a holiday and have to leave in the middle of the dinner. His life was very different from ours, and now that I have received more information from Phil it makes more sense. Phil is a retired Colonel and took the time to speak with me for hours. According to Phil, Jim was a skilled marksman and continued to work for the CIA after serving in the Vietnam War. He worked undercover in New York City. While living in Florida he owned a boat and ran clandestine missions out of Tampa and Miami, continuing to be available for the CIA. Phil said that Jim made millions in his "line of work," but all I know is that Jim died without any savings. It would seem that Mom's test with the coin when Jim was a baby came to fruition.

According to Phil, *Jim said the geometrical dimensions of Nolan's cross lead the way to further discoveries*. I am glad that Jim shared information with Phil, and I am thankful to Phil for sharing. I hope it helps in the search. Jim's stories seemed too outlandish to possibly be true, but Phil has confirmed a few of those unbelievable stories. I did not believe Jim when he would say that he could stick a shovel six inches into the ground on Oak Island and gain entrance through a secret hatch. Now I wonder if that could have been true. I think Jim and Uncle George knew things that we have yet to discover.

I appreciate Phil's friendship and support for Jim when he was alive, and the new friendship he has formed with our family. He has helped me see Jim more clearly. I believe that Jim may have been the most interesting man, and closest thing to James Bond that I have ever known, and I just did not know it at the time.

The cross surviving Jim's decision to dissolve his marriage with the mafia in New York City, or his many other adventures, is nothing short of a miracle. We acknowledge that a family gold cross is a common heirloom, and that saying to never lose sight of the cross could just as easily be a biblical warning. Very interesting about two thousand years ago the cross was seen as a symbol of shame and transformed through the years to symbolize power to many people around the world. If the cross turns out to be the key to the money pit, and the holes in it have meaning and may even represent more stones cut in half lying just beneath the surface, it is invaluable. If the cross turns out to be out of a bubble gum machine and nothing to do with Oak Island it will remain precious to us.

Joan and I have both looked on the computer for a similar design and taken the cross to jewelers. We came up empty-handed on the inter-net search, and each received reports from jewelers that could not date or define the cross. Hopefully the Lagina brothers will find an expert that can date the cross.

Chapter Twelve

"Mom" The Healer

MOM was my father's mother, her name was Rhoda Hiltz, but everyone called her Mom, even the adults. She would mother any people in need of healing. We never visited the doctor when Mom was alive. The next chapter will be the healing tonics and food recipes that we can remember, because the more I learn about what is truly healthy makes me think that the old ways are a valuable source of information.

Mom did not talk of Oak Island often. If her boys were strategizing in the kitchen, she would say, "The treasure can care for itself. You need to…" and then she would begin assigning chores. She seemed happy when she read to us from the Bible and talking about Oak Island seemed to make her sad.

Mom believed in curses and she said the McGinnis men were cursed. She believed in the power of the Mi'kmaq people and respected them. She believed if a curse was placed then it was deserved. Mom had eight children. When her twins were born, the baby boy, Charles, died. She said that George and

Bessie lost their young son in 1920 the way Daniel and Mary lost one of their sons, by drowning.

Mom confirmed her husband's story, and said they had to bury his younger brother just before Christmas. She said there was a terrible sadness over the entire island. Ambers was many years younger than Bill, and everyone adored his little brother. It was a heart-wrenching time in their life, and she was told that Henry McGinnis drowned in the pit one hundred years before in 1820.

I researched but did not find any death or marriage certificate for Henry, only his birth and christening record. If the story were true then he would have been a young teenager. There are only questions surrounding this story, but I can say with certainty that Mom was told this story by someone she believed in because she was not the type of person that would perpetuate inaccuracies. If she had seen it and said it, I would tell you that I believe it is 100% accurate. Mom had heard this story, so I cannot validate and can only share the story as I heard it.

I do not believe the validity of the story is important to the seven must die curse, because our family never said that curse existed and they believed in curses. Mom said that she heard that Daniel continued to dig after Onslow for the next ten years, and dug a third tunnel. She said he was warned by the Mi'kmaq people not to dig there. It did not sound like the brave and strong Daniel ever gave up.

Quite honestly, the story of Henry drowning does not make sense to me. Hearing this as a child I remember wondering why Daniel did not jump in and save his son, because in my mind Daniel was the bravest man on the planet. Mom explained that when a curse has been placed, things out of the ordinary would happen if all the ingredients were in place.

About the time Mom shared this story was about the same time I had gotten my first Superman comic book. I envisioned my great- treasure-hunting grandfather to be like a light-haired Superman and I called him Superdan. I could not reconcile the story, because Superdan would have saved Henry, and although I remember hearing it I do not believe it. My imaginary Superdan helped me feel brave when I walked my sisters to school through some scary neighborhoods in New Haven, Connecticut. I had an absentee father, but I felt okay because I also had a lot of uncles and an imaginary Superdan. I hope you won't laugh at a young girl's thoughts, but laugh if you must, because still to this day I am quite enamored with the adventurous life of Daniel McGinnis.

I have been struggling to remember all of Mom's words and recipes for months now, but how nice it feels when unsolicited memories of days gone by come rushing back. In February, I was standing in the kitchen with my daughters and my whole body shuddered. They laughed while asking, "what was that?" I started to say, "I don't know," but stopped midsentence as the flashback flooded in. I blurted out, "that means a spirit is visiting." They looked at me questioningly, and I repeated how Mom had explained it to me sixty years ago. Mom said that if your body had a sudden shudder more violent then just a cold shiver, that it meant a loved one's spirit was visiting. This all happened the day after Joyce left us, and we all looked around the room with tears in our eyes.

Mom died of breast cancer. She kept her chest bandaged with herbs and took care of herself, and everyone else until the very end. We would carry a secret package down to the incinerator; the apartment we lived in would light a fire in a metal bin to burn trash every day. We did not know what was in the package at the time, Joan and I would take turns taking the package down to the incinerator. One time my curiosity got the best of me and I started to unwrap the package. Mom was watching me from the window and yelled, when I came upstairs she slapped my face, it was the only time she ever hit me.

In hindsight this is a story of the strength of one incredible woman. We were just children and did not know she was sick. She did everything for us, but I do remember her not hugging us towards the end and just kissing us on the forehead. I do not know if it was painful for her to hug or if she thought what she had could be contagious. I can tell you for a fact that no one in the family knew that she was sick. I know this sounds unbelievable that the adults did not know she had breast cancer, but when she passed and her sons were called into the room, they were all shocked when the doctor showed them that one of her breasts had deteriorated. It is hard for me to believe, and I was there, but she did not let anyone know she was ill.

The day Mom left our home, I remember my Mother telling her that she had a dream that night that Mom was at our door in a white dress. Mom called for Uncle George right away, and asked him to come and get her. We cried when she left, and I remember hanging onto her skirt begging her please not to leave us, and she promised she would see us again. She said the Mi'kmaq People taught her not to say "good-bye," because it is too final and nothing in this world or the next is final. She had said when a Mi'kmaq left they would say, "I will see you again," knowing with total certainty that they would meet again either in this world or the next. She died a few days later.

One of my favorite memories of Mom was going outside and lying down in a patch of clovers and looking for hours for a four-leaf clover. Mom said they were good luck. I am not sure if she really believed in four-leaf clovers or she was just trying to keep four children entertained. We would look for hours and be lucky to find just one. Recently, I was walking and found myself in a patch of clovers and the sweet green fragrance of childhood memories with Mom and Joyce came flooding in. I bent over and picked one clover and felt a moment of reconnection when I saw that it had four leaves.

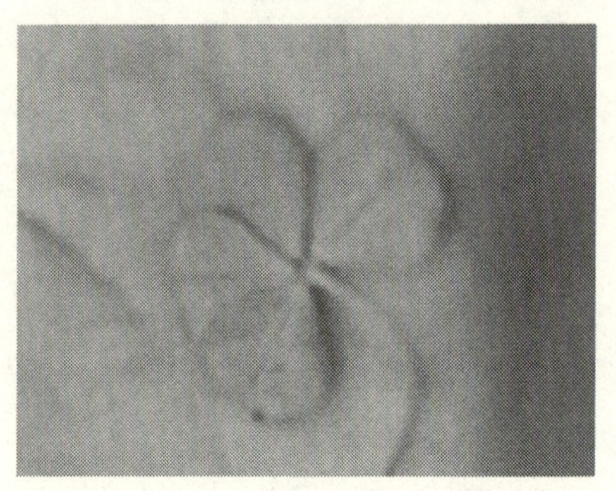

The longer I live, the less I believe in coincidences.

Joan shared her memories of Mom, S*he was gentle, loving, healing and magical. We were so fortunate to have her with us when we were little. The enduring gift she gave me is my unshakable faith in GOD. Mom taught me about GOD and the angels. She said, "An angel guards your every step." She told me I had my own guardian angel with a connection to GOD, and if I was ever in trouble I should pray with faith,* *complete and unshakable faith, and even if it took a miracle, GOD would save me or maybe HE would let my angel do it.*

At Mom's funeral, we three were getting rowdy so Mommy gave us Bazooka bubble gum if we promised to be good, you know the one wrapped in a funny with a fortune at the bottom? Oh yeah! Well, I promised faithfully and happily popped mine in my mouth, looked at my funny and then at my fortune... It read, "An angel guards your every step."

That is when I realized and understood in my young mind that Mom's promise was true. She would always be with me. Mommy carefully tucked the wrapper inside a cellophane wrapper, and I saved it. I still have it.

Chapter Thirteen

Mom's Healing Recipes

Mom credited the Mi'kmaqs with some of her healing knowledge. Mom would talk about the original people of Nova Scotia with a great appreciation, and when we were young we called them the MickeyMacs. It is a shame to recall that Native People did not always have the respect that all people deserve, but that was not the case in our home. Mom taught us many things she learned. The word Mi'kmaq is a word from their language that translates into English to mean kin-friends. I don't know if the people of Nova Scotia had a name for themselves, but Mom said they greeted the European settlers calling them kin-friends, and the settlers abbreviated that word to Mi'kmaq. When I think of the word MickeyMacs, it brings a smile to my face.

'Modern medicine' has become unhealthy for some, and healing from a pre-pharmaceutical era may become useful information. It is recommended that before trying any new healthy additions, you consult your doctor. Mom would cut cloth patches of one-inch by one-inch squares and sew them together and stuff them with ingredients. I remember different smells depending on our ailments, and when I get a whiff of anything with eucalyptus in it I remember the white patch I wore to school. My sister Joan had some allergies and wore a patch that smelled differently.

If we were sick, our patch smelled different and was bigger. She would collect and boil sticks and leaves and make a sack out of old pillows and lay it on our chests if we got a cold. I do not remember what she gathered, so I looked up old healing recipes that involved sticks and found this: "ektjimpisun." The ingredients of this medicine are: "wikpe" (alumwillow), "waqwonuminokse" (wild black cherry), "kastuk" (ground hemlock), and "kowotmonokse" (red spruce).
http://www.gov.pe.ca/photos/original/AborigCC_2015.pdf
I do not know if that is the ingredients she used, but whatever Mom did, it worked fast and we never went to the doctors.

Mom reading tealeaves was a real treat. She would make us a cup of tea and then we would tip the cup over, and she would show us a bird and other things. It felt really special, and she mostly did it when we started to not feel well. I have no idea how she came up with remedies from that, but she did and they worked.

She would hang some type of herb above the front and back door to guard our home, and I remember how safe it made me feel at the time. If someone came to visit that she did not want to return she would throw salt in his or her path. I have not actually tried this one, but Mom claimed that it would deter them from returning.

In our bathroom was kept the toothbrush, the hairbrush and the dry brush. Mom would brush our skin every night from our toes towards our heart, it would make my skin tingly and itchy. It was hard to stand still when she moved the brush in short movements because it tickled. I did not know at the time that she was moving my lymphatic system, but I will remind you that my sisters and I never once visited a doctor while Mom was living with us.

Mom made the smallest imprint on the earth and the largest imprint on my world. She put a wooden crate outside the window in the cold months, so we did not need to use the icebox in the winter and buy ice from the iceman. Mom would repurpose every container for something. Mom saved every rag and cut up old coats and dishcloths for a braiding pile. She taught us all how to braid and when it was long enough, she would sew a rug out of the braided rags. I wish I had saved one of the patchwork quilts she had sewn for us.

She wasted nothing. As a child I thought she spooned out the cod liver oil because no one else on the planet wanted it, and she never let anything go to waste. She would give us a spoonful of Cod Liver Oil on our way out the door to school. It was awful; about second period I would taste it again. Now that I have grown and know how good fish oil is for me, I still avoid it and only like to do things that are healthy and taste good too. The honey cures I enjoyed. She used honey for everything, inside and out. Mom would paste the sticky paste on our knees to take away scars so we would grow up and have beautiful legs.

Mom loved to read to us from the Bible; she was not just spiritual, she was strong and knowledgeable. She said the Bible was full of remedies. She used Hydrogen Peroxide, and I have just seen in the past couple of years that Hydrogen Peroxide is beneficial.

Mom would put the brown bottle of hydrogen peroxide outside in the winter; after it froze she would pour out the little bit of liquid left into a glass jar that was marked as poison. I can remember watching my Mom and thinking she looked like a scientist. We were never allowed to touch this and she would use a dropper to put a drop in water to drink, and a couple drops to soak our feet in. The water did not have much of a taste, so I did not mind that as much as I hated the cod liver oil. I like to try everything that could make me feel good, especially if it does not taste bad.

A few years ago I read a health book called, "The One Minute Miracle," by Madison Cavanaugh, and was surprised to see that hydrogen peroxide used to be taken internally. According to this book, "over 170 years ago, when India was still a British colony, the Indian people found that hydrogen peroxide added in minute amounts to drinking water cured a variety of illnesses from the minor ones like colds and flu all the way to serious ones like cholera and malaria. Because its use threatened the British monopoly drug sales, they hired a news reporter disguised as a doctor to fabricate a story." Greed has been the reason for misinformation throughout history, but undermining other people's health and vitality to turn a profit is unconscionable.

It is not impossible to order food grade hydrogen peroxide, but it is volatile and dangerously strong at that percentage. I prefer to use 3% food grade hydrogen peroxide that I have found at organic markets. I have found out that it is not good to eat any green leafy vegetables for a few hours before or after drinking drops of hydrogen peroxide diluted in water. It is an interesting health idea, oxygenating the body. Anything that gives me more energy and does not taste bad, I like.

I was the first of the children to get chicken pox, and Mom made my sisters catch it and then she put us in a dark room for days. She hung blankets on the windows and we could not see sunlight. None of us have scars, but I am not sure what the darkness did for us. If we got itchy she would spray us with Apple Cider Vinegar. She would keep a batch mixed of one cup of water to ¼ cup of Apple Cider Vinegar. She would keep this spray handy for mosquito bites. Joan was allergic to mosquitoes and would swell up after being bitten, and apple cider vinegar would help her sensitive skin.

OTHER WAYS TO USE APPLE CIDER VINEGAR

Dilute a shot glass full of apple cider vinegar with a cup of water and drink a glass everyday (1 T apple cider vinegar to 8 oz. of water). Always rinse your mouth with fresh water after you drink it. When we got a sore throat, Mom would mix six parts of water to one part apple cider vinegar for us to gargle with. We would try to gargle for at least 30 seconds and she would have us rinse with water and do it again. It would burn and make my mouth water after I spit it out, but that usually took care of the sore throat. If the sore throat persisted or when we got a cold she would pick greens and herbs and make a steam place at the stove for us to smell.

Apple Cider Vinegar Hair rinse. I did not like rinsing my hair in vinegar when I was young, because if it got in my eyes it would burn, but I just recently read an article about how good it is to rinse the shampoo build-up out of your hair and leave

it shiny, so I started rinsing my hair again with Mom's recipe. Seventy years later, I am wise enough to keep my head back till the vinegar is completely rinsed out of my hair.
4 parts water
to 1 part apple cider vinegar (less for dry & more for oily hair)
If you want to hide the odor of apple cider vinegar use 3-4 drops of lavender or any other essential oil, I like the smell of apple cider vinegar and marjoram.
Mix ingredients in a glass spray bottle or a glass jar and dump it on. Massage over wet hair and work through from roots to ends. Rinse out.

If you are interested in homemade shampoo, Mom would mix one part of baking soda to three parts of warm water and mix well. She would massage in gently and let it sit for a minute or two before washing it out with plain water. I have done a little research and do this only once a week to clean shampoo residue off of my hair and it leaves it silky soft. If a baking soda shampoo is used too often it can thin out the hair.

When you look at her picture you can see that Mom had a natural beauty and did not wear much make-up. She would cut open a beet and dab it on her cheeks and lips, she was naturally beautiful inside and out. She had such a genuine and kind spirit and is missed everyday.

"Mom," the healer.

We did silly things like pick buttercups and hold them under our chin. She used the flowers for a medicine and I think that was her way to get us to pick them for her. She would collect the plants from us and she would smash the flowers and leaves of the buttercups. She would use this if someone in the house had a headache, and I think this happened a lot because there may have been a few hangovers to be cured. For all aches and pains she would administer a root broth that would help within minutes, and the recipe is in the next chapter.

The children did not get the buttercup recipe, if we had a headache she would squeeze our ear lobe and for allergies she would squeeze the top of Joan's ears. She would spend five minutes every day touching our faces, and she called it tapping for a smile. I always felt better and more relaxed after she did this. She would start tapping on my chin, and then under my lips and under my nose. She would tap her fingers lightly under my eyes and then on my eyebrows; she would end it by tapping on my head. Sometimes, I take the time to do this for myself and think of her. If you are so inclined, try it for yourself.

Chapter Fourteen

MOM'S COOK BOOK

Mom did not waste anything. I have grown to be as dissipative as the majority, but it is good to know how to be resourceful if hard times were to ever hit. She could make an entire meal out of a few scraps. Every meal was based with greens. We would pick dandelion greens for her, before the flower opened up or else they would be bitter, and she would use the leaves and stems and fry them up and pile them in the center of the plate. We were eating inexpensively at the time but with all the latest food discoveries, we were eating healthy. Mom would not cut the ends off the vegetables, because she would say the best part is at the end. It is uncertain if she believed the roots and vines were really the best part, or if we just had to use every part to feed everyone in the house.

'Daily Greens,' painted by Jean McGinnis

In one house we lived in, there was an apple tree in the backyard and she made pies, still to this day I have never tasted an apple pie as wonderful as Mom's. She would soak the apples overnight in a brown sauce; I have experimented but have not yet perfected Mom's Apple Pie. We also made applesauce, apple fritters, and the peels went into a jug for vinegar. I can share the vinegar drink recipe, because I helped her make the apple cider vinegar and we would drink it everyday.

We could make a whole gallon from just the peels. Joan and I would climb up the tree and pick the apples and throw them down for Joyce to put in a bag, while Mom would be yelling up "Be Careful" and "That's High Enough." My sisters and I would get to taste-test the apples, because Mom liked to mix sweet apples and add some bitter and sharp-tasting apples. Mom used our large jugs of vinegar for everything from tonics to cleaning. I still use her recipe to this day. If you do not want to make your own purchase the cloudy Apple Cider Vinegar from the grocery store that says 'unfiltered.' The clear apple cider vinegar does not have the powerful health benefits.

APPLE CIDER VINEGAR

Ingredients

Scraps from 10 apples, or 5 whole apples

water

Equipment

1-gallon jar

Large rubber band

Instructions

Before you can make your raw apple cider vinegar, you must first make hard apple cider. Wash the apples and coarsely chop into pieces no smaller than 1 inch. Remove the stems and the apple seeds. Put the chopped apples into a 1-gallon glass jar. The chopped apples should at least fill half the container. Pour in room temperature natural spring water until the chopped apples are completely covered, while leaving a couple of inches at the top. Now, cover the top of the glass jar with cheesecloth and put a large rubber band to hold it in place.

Leave on the counter for about one week, gently mixing twice a day. Bubbles will begin to form as the sugar ferments. Smelling this happen brings back delicious memories for me. In about one week, when the apple scraps no longer float and sink to the bottom of the jar, the hard apple cider is ready. Taste it to see if it is the right acidity level for you, if it is too strong dilute it with some water. Strain out the apple scraps and pour the hard apple cider into clean glass jars. Store in the cabinet or pantry out of direct sunlight. Raw apple cider vinegar doesn't go bad, but if you find a growth on top just strain it and dilute with a bit of water if the taste has become too strong.

Later, I learned that even though this tastes acidic, it is actually one of the best ways to make your body alkaline. Apple Cider Vinegar turns alkaline when mixed with your stomach acid. Today we know disease cannot form in an alkaline environment, THANKS MOM!

RECIPES: How to sneak in the APPLE CIDER VINEGAR

I drink a shot of apple cider vinegar a day diluted in a full glass of water. If you do not like the taste of this vinegar drink, get your shot glass of vinegar everyday in your body by mixing it with other things, tomato juice covers up the vinegar bite. A nice salad can mask the taste of the vinegar, while still delivering the health benefits.

Mom would make a cold dish of broccoli, stewed tomatoes, apple cider vinegar and garlic. This is very easy to make, but best if it sits overnight. Put a can of whole tomatoes and garlic in a pan and simmer till the garlic softens, add bite-size chunks of broccoli and cook just till crisp-tender. Let it cool and put it in a glass jar with 6 T Apple Cider Vinegar. This is a delicious diet snack because it is filling and packs a nutritious punch. Tomatoes cover up the vinegar taste and the dish has a slight taste of being pickled, without the whole canning process.

MOM'S BEAN SALAD

This dish was always different colors, she used whatever beans she had; green, waxed, pinto, garbanzo, kidney, white or black beans. She would add some chopped onion, celery and garlic mixed with apple cider vinegar and honey to taste. This gets better as it sits overnight and the tastes blend together. The smell of our icebox would make my mouth water.

BREAD: Mom would make homemade bread every morning, and sometimes I would help.

It is easy just add the following three dry ingredients

5 cups flour

4 tsp. baking powder

1 tsp. salt

Add the wet ingredients, 3 cups liquid (2 ½ cups water and ½ cup oil). Be aware and informed when selecting oil. Anything that is "partially hydrogenated," is not good for your body. This can be found in canola, corn, cottonseed and soybean oil, be aware that some manufacturers try to sneak that in a lot of processed food. Healthy options include, but are not limited to; coconut oil, olive oil, avocado oil, walnut oil and grape seed oil. Monounsaturated fats are the "good fats" that help to regulate cholesterol and help your body absorb antioxidants and nutrients. Making healthy food choices have just a few simple rules of quality water, good oil and real food that your body can recognize.

Directions for making bread:

Roll out the mixed soft dough into a bread pan and cut into squares with a floured knife.

Bake at 300 degrees for 45 minutes

WHITE GRAVY

My favorite was when she would make a white gravy to pour over the bread. She could make so much, with so few ingredients for so many people. Her white gravy was just whatever bits were left in the frying pan mixed with flour and water. I started out appreciating white gravy, but ended up later in life owning an Italian Deli, I could have any meat I wanted, and I still loved that white gravy.

BREAD PUDDING

Any bread scraps would go into a container to make bread pudding. She saved it until there was enough stale bread to fill the pan.

Ingredients

6 eggs

3 cups of milk

Homemade vanilla about 1T.

Half a cup of syrup (karo, maple or molasses) Put the bread in mixture in fridge over night and pour into greased pan and bake at 350 degrees for about one hour.

ROOT BROTH

Turmeric and ginger root broth was what we would drink every time we had the beginnings of an ache or pain of any kind. It is very soothing for a sore throat. Mom would boil Turmeric root, Ginger root and a whole head of Garlic, and she would store it in a jar in the icebox. I still drink a lot of this, but when I make it, I add cilantro. The cilantro gives it a refreshing flavor, but I do not transfer the cilantro to the jar and it keeps nicely for a few days. I drink it cold instead of tea and find it not only thirst quenching but also satiating.

She made a lot with cabbage leaves. She would half fry and half boil cabbage with garlic cloves and pile our plates full. The leaves would turn a golden brown and have a sweet taste.

CABBAGE

Ingredients:

A head of cabbage cut into quarters.

½ cup of olive oil

Add both to a covered pot and fry on low. When some of the leaves start to turn brown and caramelize, add the garlic cloves. Be careful not to burn the garlic, and add a cup of water after the garlic had a chance to flavor the oil (add more oil if you need). Cover and simmer till leaves are soft. This has a sweet delicious taste. Enjoy.

STUFFED CABBAGE

Broccoli recipe: 6 cloves of chopped garlic

One head of broccoli - diced

One can of crushed tomatoes (I like Marzanno)

2 cups cooked rice.

4 fresh basil leaves

Put garlic in pan with a can of Marzanno crushed tomatoes, let it simmer to most of juice is gone and garlic are soft, add in broccoli till they are just crisp-tender. Mix in with the cooked rice to make balls and wrap steamed cabbage leaves. Place in a shallow baking pan and fill with an inch of tomato juice, or you can use the turmeric-ginger broth. Bake at 350° for 30 min.

CORN FRITTERS

She made cornbread in a frying pan on a wood stove. My favorite was Mom's special corn fritters, they are such a treat and are easy to make.

Ingredients

One can of corn, or one cup of corn cut off the cob

3 T of flour

Half a cup of milk, salt and pepper to taste.

Spoon a mound of mixture into hot, high quality oil and flip when golden brown. The corn fritters hardly ever make it to the dinner table because the kids come in the kitchen and sneak them when I am frying.

Chapter Fifteen

The Facts of Oak Island Stand Strong

I hope you enjoyed reading the variety of stories shared by my mother and aunts. What came across in all of the stories from them, their uncles and grandparents, is a connection to something deeper. The foundation is a strong belief that Oak Island is something worth the investment of valuable time.

Daniel McGinnis made the search a priority in his life, even though it returned so little value to him. John McGinnis was said to feel a lack of accomplishment, because he never found what he searched his entire life for. Lee Lamb described Bob Restall as being obsessed, and he had the support of his son Bobby to drive that obsession. Fred Nolan led a relentless pursuit and discovered the cross made of conical boulders. Dan Blankenship has been very focused for half a century documenting his many efforts, along with his son David keeping him on target. The Lagina brothers have fueled the fire for people around the world to keep searching.

These men stood as strong as the towering Red Oak Trees, but they were planted in sandy soil. The search seems to come so close to grasping something tangible, only to have it fall through like sand through an hourglass. I tried not to impose my own guesswork in this book, and just relay the facts as I heard them, but the Oak trees are so unusual that I just cannot resist. The way the Oak Trees grew were so very different from all the other Oaks in the area. They shot straight up, with no branches along the trunk till the tree explodes in a wide canopy. These trees remind me of the trees drawn in the cartoons by Dr. Seuss, and they look out of place in Nova Scotia.

Smith's Cove.

Smith's Cove, showing the old-fashioned hoisting whim near the shore

This old photo was uncovered by the oakislandcompendium.ca

The existence of these unusual trees inspired me to search for reasons why it would grow in this unique way. I found if Oak trees are planted in sandy soil they grow a very deep taproot, and they do this relatively quickly. Sandy soil allows the Oak tree to shoot straight up and straight down. If you look at the straight line of trees that lined Smith's Cove you may wonder if they were planted with a purpose. It is my opinion that the Oak trees were planted to reinforce the area underground.

If the Oak trees were planted for the strength of their root systems, that could explain the curse of treasure not being found until all the Oak trees are gone from the island. As the trees were chopped down and the roots began to rot, I wonder if whatever they were planted to secure is now undermined and accessible. I believe the namesake of the island had a purpose for being there.

When people start guessing, it can take away from the facts. My red oak theory of the roots being used to reinforce the tunnels may be a reach. There is a simpler possibility, and that is someone wanted to have Gloucester Island stand out in Mahone Bay from the 360 other islands as Oak Island. A westbound ship would see the towering red canopy in September. I wondered how long a tree would have to grow to tower above evergreens. A formula was developed and used by the International Society of Arboriculture to predict

and determine a tree's age.
http://forestry.about.com/od/silviculture/a/Estimating-A-Trees-Age.htm
Applying this formula to a red oak tree of Oak Island, estimates the tree to be 171 years old. The reference point for size came from two men standing next to the base of the tree in the picture above from oakislandcompendium.ca .

The fascination with Oak Island has continued long after the Oak trees have been gone, but there have been many discoveries that inspire people to keep searching. Men began the obsession with Oak Island before there was any idea of the elaborate floodgates. Daniel and his crew were oblivious for years to the roar of the sea, as it waited at bay to devour any man whose shovel dug too deep. I imagine the hardship of their search during the final fruitless days of late autumn, when the blustering wind chased after them through the leafless branches of the Oak trees. I think of them sitting in their cabins, empty-handed for another cold and long winter.

I wonder about what we now know as the underwater gates and reflect on the construction process for the original diggers of the tunnel. I consider the possibility of the ocean water constantly applying pressure, waiting for the moment that will allow the floodwaters the chance to enter. Even more inconceivable, is the possibility that the gates were constructed in a way that there is no pressure on the entrance until the shovel strikes the pre-calculated depth.

Many people question this tunnel system. I claim no wisdom in the matter of fate or destiny, but have an unrelenting belief that the treasure held enough value to warrant the manual labor invested in hiding it. I believe it will eventually be exposed, and after it has been unearthed it is my personal opinion that we will be even more impressed with whoever left the original deposit.

Oak Island is notorious for many unanswered questions, but we are certain that the men who buried this were successful at building a dam that held long enough to construct the drain system. Since the original and successful dam, there have been two attempts that I am aware of to try and construct a dam and both have failed. Most people reading this are probably aware of the construction details, but I will quote below so you know the size and magnitude. *"This drain system resembled the fingers of a hand and was spread out over 145ft of beach. Each finger was a man made [sic] channel with layers of rocks, eel grass and coconut fibers, an excellent filtration system to keep silt and sand out and allow water to flow freely."*
http://littletwotwo.hubpages.com/hub/Oak-Island-Money-Pi

Charles Barkhouse can give you a detailed description of the complexity of this tunnel system; it will definitely make you wonder who, what, when, and HOW? And of course, WHY? The original construction was so masterfully created that it makes me wonder if a woman could have designed the system, as in 'Mother Nature.'

I researched all the possibilities I could think of, even the ones that were not popular with my family. My children's teacher, from Gifft Hill School, V.I. did a study of the rock formations on Oak Island. He concluded, "The stratum beneath Oak Island primarily consists of limestone and anhydrite. This type of geology is associated with the formation of caverns, salt domes and sink holes." The possibility of natural formations beneath Oak Island neither disproves, nor proves what we are all seeking. If any of the pits prove to be natural, it does not make Oak Island any less amazing. It does not negate the stone markers in the shape of the 'tree of life,' or Nolan's cross. If the tunnel system was not entirely created by man, it just proves that man was ingenious enough to utilize nature when he designed the finger drains. Oak Island may have been selected because of the natural properties it does possess.

Even though there are no written records from 1795, we do know that the way the pit appeared was sufficient motivation for McGinnis, Smith and Vaughn to dedicate their lives to digging. You now are aware of the fact that enough information was uncovered to compel five generations of McGinnis men to continue searching. All of the pieces of the Oak Island puzzle are fascinating. I hope that once the construction is understood the missing pieces will fall into place, and this will all make sense.

South Shore Cove 2015

If the drains tied to the money pit are interesting to you, you will want to read a story that my cousin, Kelly Hancock, published on his blog:

http://www.oakislandcompendium.ca/blockhouse-blog/do-ice-holes-on-oak-islands-south-shore-hint-at-flood-traps

Below is a quote he included from Dan Blankenship, giving us all reason to keep exploring.

1979 "It was bitter cold and the bay had frozen over with about 2 to 3inches of ice. We were working enlarging our shaft from the existing 2-inch casing to about an 8-foot diameter steel and concert shaft. In order to conserve fuel we would shut the pump off each night, and restart pumping very early in the morning. At that time, it took about 1 1/2 to 2 hours to dewater. It was while the shaft had reached the level of about 105 to 110 ft. that we noticed the phenomenon of the spaced holes in the ice. When we first noticed them, there were four sets of holes widely spaced of two holes each. These holes were quite symmetrical in that they contained two holes each of about 25 to 30 feet and the holes aligned themselves at right angle to the beach, in other words, one hole behind the other. The hole to the right apparently was the most active and it enlarged itself to compass both small holes

At that time it was assumed that we had

reached a level of man-made flood tunnels,
out daily pumping dewatered these areas.
When the pumps were shut off for the night
it allowed these areas to fill up and the
compressed air found its way thru the system
where the warm air bubbles prevented the
direct area above them to freeze.
This conclusion seemed to be confirmed this
last February when the same phenomenon
occurred again. The ice had formed on the bay, but
not as thick as in 1979. We were working in our
shaft at about 127 feet when our shaft broke
on our pump and the area recharged with ocean
water. The next day the ice holes
appeared in the same location.

- Dan Blankenship, Nov. 9th 1987

Thank You Dan, for all your hard work and for taking such good notes.

I can envision a skilled and very motivated group of people building a dam and creating the finger drains, but I cannot imagine how they connected it to 200 feet from shore. Maybe that is tied into a naturally occurring system. There are many unanswered questions, but just because we do not yet know how does not negate their extraordinary existence.

Chapter Sixteen

Trespassing on Oak Island

Our trip to Oak Island was a nostalgic family vacation. We drove from Connecticut and took the car ferry to Nova Scotia in 2009. We traveled to Chester and stayed in the Atlantica Hotel in the hopes of going to Oak Island one of the days of our stay. We stood on the shore looking across the causeway with such a yearning but did not see a way to get closer. I had called the Oak Island tourist number ahead of time, but we had just missed an Oak Island open house held the month before, and they said to try again next year. I called all the numbers I could find to see if we could meet with someone and talk about Oak Island, but did not succeed.

The trip was too exciting to be disappointed. My mother was thrilled to be going back and Aunt Joyce came along not expecting much from the trip, but enjoying the family time. We got a little closer to the island by taking a ride on a boat called "Mrs. Wonderful," the captain was awesome and he got the boat as close as he dared, but Oak Island remained just out of our reach.

Joyce and Jean on the back of the boat "Mrs. Wonderful"

On our last day in Nova Scotia, my mother sighed out loud a little as she looked longingly across the bay, and my Uncle Marty said come on Jeanie we are sneaking onto Oak Island. I wanted to go, but he said someone might have to bail them out.

They came back exhilarated, and sat with the rest of the family by a campfire overlooking Oak Island and told us all about their adventure. Everyone was surprised that Jean went, no one sitting there had ever known her to break the rules. We asked Uncle Marty how he got her to sneak across the causeway? He said he had to coax her past every "No Trespassing" sign they came to, and there were quite a few. He said it took a long time with Jean walking so slowly, but they made it to a marker that they could see the name McGinnis on, and that made her forget how nervous she was. Jean took the picture below of the sign.

She was thrilled to pieces to see the foundation of Daniel's cabin, and said that single moment was worth the next few terrifying and embarrassing minutes. A car came speeding towards them, with a trail of dust behind and came to a screeching halt. A woman got out of the car, in all her fullness, and began yelling.

Uncle Marty stood strong, and he said Jean got really close to him, like she wanted to jump in his pocket. She said she thought of her brave, late-great- treasure-hunting grandfather and mustered up enough courage to say, "we did not come to steal any treasure, and our name is McGinnis." That seemed to make the lady angrier. She screamed that she did not care what their name was. Marty asked the woman if there is any land still owned by a McGinnis on the island, but she just said, "Leave Now!" As they were being not so kindly escorted off the island, they attracted the attention of Dan Blankenship, and he gently informed them that it is a private island and explained that it is not safe to allow trespassers.

Jean said she was honored to meet Mr. Blankenship, in both 2009 and 2015. During our recent visit we were invited in Dan Blankenship's home on Oak Island. The very end of the last episode in season three on the "Curse of Oak Island," you can hear Jean and Dan laughing as the camera fades out, she was reminding him of the first time they met six years earlier.

The last day in Nova Scotia in 2009 was one to remember, and the evening turned into a memorable one with its clear skies and beautiful moonrise. My daughter, Jeanie, named after her grandmother, was the first to spot the moon rising. It did not look like the moon at first, only a thin orange sliver on the horizon. As it rose, we saw she was right and the moon made a glowing cross out of light - literally. I am drawn to the full moon and have taken my family on many hikes to get to the best place to watch the moonrise, and I have yet to see one similar to that night. A cross of light on the moon may be a common occurrence that far north, but it is the one and only time I have seen it.

We sat together for hours that evening talking about our moonstruck family and sharing their outrageous stories. The night sky looked like someone had thrown a handful of confetti in the air and was nothing short of spectacular. My mother said, “how in the world can anyone think human beings are the only life in the universe, with all those billions of stars and billions more planets revolving around them?”

I know it will be futile to try and explain how many bright lights lit the dark sky, but I will try for all the people who have not yet made it to a desolate location on our planet and looked up. It is difficult to compare a sky with light pollution that has maybe a couple hundred stars visible, with the sky that lay before me. As I looked into the night, I could not tell if there was more dark space or more white stars. My eyes tried to focus on the many layers of distant light, and I think there were more light spots than there was dark space.

Someone said "look!" and we saw a shooting star and all made a wish on it. We decided to wish that we could get on Oak Island and explore some day. Exactly six years later, almost to the day, we received a very generous invitation from the Lagina brothers to visit Oak Island. The McGinnis family has decided that if we are ever sitting together and see another shooting star, we are going to wish to find the buried treasure of Oak Island. Wish Big, My Fellow Believers, and then live happily until your wish comes true.

Chapter Seventeen

Special Invitation To Oak Island

We had the 5th, 6th and 7th generation of Daniel McGinnis on Oak Island during September 2015: the three McGinnis sisters, I am the 6th generation and I brought my oldest daughter. We asked before we came if we would be allowed to explore Oak Island, when they answered "yes," this was a wish upon a star come true. There are no words in English to describe the feeling we had walking around Oak Island.

The Lagina brothers were both two gentlemen, so much so that it almost felt like we had gone back in time. The area of the McGinnis cabin was beautiful with a spectacular view. We walked around the beach stone foundation and I noticed there was no area where a well would have been. I have lived on an island for years that has no fresh water, and we collect rainwater on the roof that goes into a cistern, so it is natural for me to notice water sources. When I asked how they collected water, my mother said she remembered a water barrel that was next to a big outside pot used for cooking.

She looked out at the ocean and said she remembered Grandpa Bill saying when Daniel and Mary moved here there was a large fresh water hole with a dam. He said it was due east of the cabin along the north shore beach, and she pointed in the direction we were heading anyway. This was starting to make sense, because when it does not rain on my island we can buy water, but I could not think of a reason why anyone would start a family on an island with no fresh water source in the summer months.

Jean said, "I'm not sure what I was anticipating to feel on Oak Island, but I felt my heart going so fast in my chest, and I almost could not speak because I felt so busy soaking it all in." You would think it is not that big a deal to see your grandparents' house, but everything about Oak Island is magnified. I personally do not think the secrets of Oak Island are limited to the one area designated as the money pit, because the entire island had a supercharged feeling to it.

Jean said, "Crossing the causeway for the second time was so much more exciting than the first time, because this time I was welcomed." Joan said, "Walking on the island was the thrill of a lifetime for me." There was an aroma of anticipation as we set foot on Oak Island. The Lagina brothers were true to their word and after answering their questions in the war room, we were given a car, a very patient driver named Ryan, and a free pass to go anywhere on Oak Island.

If I try to tune out the rational thoughts and focus on the senses, I find myself overwhelmed with confidence of there being something special on Oak Island. I am not going to say it was spooky, because that is not the right word, but it is the closest feeling I can relay to try to explain a wave that came over me in a few areas. I did not want to run from it, so it was different from feeling afraid yet similar to fear. Most of the island was light and bright and beautiful, but there were two locations that were dark and sent chills through my body.

Echoing in my mind were our family stories of Daniel telling us to embrace fear. He taught many generations that to feel afraid is a natural reaction, so recognize and accept it, but then continue on to conquer it. Passing from this realm to the next is wrought with fear, because of the uncertain elements, but there are stories and signs that could help us know it is just different. We all have the choice to either embrace the teachings, or ignore them and figure out our own way. Thus is free will. I tried to be open to anything unusual, and was hoping to see Daniel telling me I was searching in the wrong spot, but I did not.

We are grateful to the Lagina brothers for many things, and one is their sense of timing. We had tried to contact them earlier, but their response and request came at the perfect time for us. They brought the three sisters from the West Coast, the Northeast and the South for their last earthly adventure together. We would like to believe what our great-great-great-great Uncle John said about the afterlife being the ultimate adventure, than we could picture Joyce on an exciting journey. I do believe that Joyce knows all the answers now, and she knows what lies beneath Oak Island. How ironic that the skeptic has it all figured out before the believer even has a clue.

This book started with Joyce and it will end with Joyce, she was such a sweetheart and left this world on Valentine's Day. As Joyce took her last breath my sister Raina was on one side of her bed and Jean was on the other. Joyce turned her precious face and said, "Don't cry Jeanie," and she did not inhale again. Jean was not able to embrace her words and cried for days, sobbing that if only she knew for sure she was okay. A couple of mornings after Valentine's Day, my mother saw an owl in a water oak tree. She collects owls, but had not seen one in her yard before. She walked out of the screen porch, and the owl flew down from the branch to stand at her feet. My sister watched breathless from the porch, not wanting to scare it away, but it did not seem afraid. The owl just stood there and looked up for a few minutes and then flew away. If anyone catches Jean feeling sad now, we remind here of that sign. We can just hear Joyce say, “I sent you an owl, Jeanie. What more do you need to know I am well?” I think of the Mi’kmaqs and say with confidence, “I will see you again.”

Chapter Eighteen

Oak Island is Intoxicating

I believe if I feel it. Just because I do not see something does not dissuade my belief. To feel the love of a kindred spirit, and believe in that unseen life-changing force, is transformational. The logical evidence for Oak Island, although quite intriguing, is weak for me compared to the overwhelming feeling and intuition. Once I made it to Oak Island my gut feeling and five senses supported my belief in something deeper.

I wonder if the past two centuries of my descendants where in love with Oak Island, or maybe with what Oak Island could deliver. Either way, there was a common passion. Could the money pit be a waste of time if it inspired mad, passionate, extraordinary love of searching?

I have considered the hardships of the original families living on Oak Island. I have lived on an island since the beginning of the 21st century, but it is incomparable because my island has grocery stores and car ferries. Although I have watched some of the residents suffer from an affliction called "Rock Fever," to get over it they have to take a trip off-island. Did the early settlers feel isolated, or was it more of a camaraderie that Oak Island life instilled? In the records, I noticed that John McInnis (Daniel's oldest son) married Jane Vaughn in 1817, so I am guessing that at least two members of the original families did not mind island life.

Hardships of Island Life, Painted by Jean McGinnis 2015

As I thought of all the many and varied, wild and passionate people that have searched this island, like President Roosevelt and John Wayne, it made me wonder if other treasure hunts enticed as many souls. I found that there are other treasures throughout the world that have been lost with an approximate location, and these treasures have an actual amount they are worth, yet the search for them does not come close to the Oak Island quest.

During the end of World War II, Nazis sunk containers and various other objects into Lake Toplitz. The containers at the bottom of the lake may contain art wonders such as the legendary Amber Room Panels from the 18th century. There have been searches for sunken treasure, but nothing comes close to the treasure hunt on Oak Island for the past 220+ years. Oak Island has planted seeds of obsession with so many, but offered absolutely no idea of what treasure lies below.

The purpose of this book was to call anyone with information forward, in the hopes that sharing information could help point out the right direction. This has already begun, just this week an historian reached out to me and I am fascinated with her project. I asked her for a quote about her work, "I am working with a Templar record and have found a connection to Oak Island. The interconnections established by this discovery have led to a breakthrough in the mystery of Oak Island. The Templar connection will be described in the forthcoming book that will conclude six years of research." I am looking forward to reading this with much anticipation.

We all have many questions, and I will leave you with mine. I will share this idea in the hopes that someone can take it further. There were many homesteads on Oak Island throughout the 1800's, and that no one used the stones of the triangle is surprising. The triangle with a rounded bottom resembles a sextant. Could the H+0 stone be a marking point?

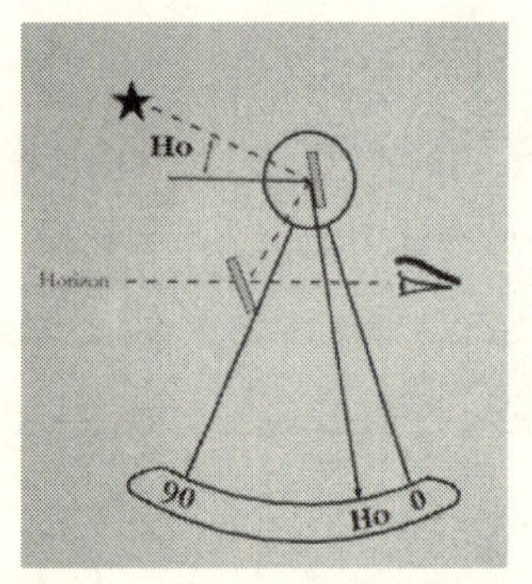

We did not take this book or our small part in the search lightly, and went through a hypnotist to try and retrieve information. It is hard to know what is wishful thinking and what is delivered from another realm. A session brought me to a stone in the remains of the foundation of the McGinnis cabin. After taking the round stone I found myself immediately out to sea in a rowboat. I had asked for answers to access the treasure of Oak Island, but found only questions. In order to find answers we may have to reach for mystical levels of understanding, similar to the Templars open-minded belief system.

We hope you enjoyed the stories, as for me compiling this did nothing to quench my curiosity. In fact, hearing from some people about my family, actually instilled more questions because they brought validity to some of the stories. As far as Lindsay and Jim are concerned, time has slowly revealed through the years some justifiable reasons for their covert lifestyle. It leaves me with more questions than answers. I urge the Lagina brothers on now, even more than ever, to find answers. Hopefully in Season Four.

Until the truth unfolds, let all those bitten by the Oak Island bug continue to enjoy the search. I believe in following your gut and relying on your intuition. People have grown dependent on information from the Internet and may not hear the internal voices as loudly as they did centuries ago. There is a deep assuredness that comes with following your intuitive guide; it is hard to build that confidence level with online informational searches. Information is power, so I think it is worth the time to take a moment and check in with your body and become internally in touch. If you find yourself obsessed with Oak Island, ask yourself, "Is it just about solving a mystery, or is it more?"

Oak Island Bug Symptom Relief:
If you experience an insatiable appetite for any information about Oak Island, you may want to count yourself as one of

the many held firmly in its grip. I think the only cure will be when the treasure has been found, but until then, the key to finding relief is to realize the difference in interest versus passion. I am interested in Greek mythology and constellations, but Oak Island feels like more than an interest. The closest feeling I can relate it to is being head over heels in love. The connection when two soul mates meet and fall in love, the magnetic attraction is unexplainable. For a time you want to eat, sleep and breathe that other soul; similar to that insatiable feeling, I cannot get enough of Oak Island. I believe the island holds the people with a deep connection. I am passionately in love with Oak Island.

One way to find relief is to enjoy the blogs and posts of people who have done research on Oak Island. Another way is to connect with other passionate people on the many Facebook Group Pages. If you have any information you would like to share, please e-mail **OstrichFreeDiet@gmail.com**.

After our visit to Nova Scotia I began working on an Oak Island Love Story, a romantic fiction based on the many stories I heard and my own island life experience. A light read until the serious, summer digging begins and "The Curse of Oak Island," brings us exciting news.
Enjoy the first chapter.

Untitled

Book

Epilogue: Oak Island is not just romantic, it is necromantic.

Chapter One: The Meeting

On the first day of August 1795, my girlfriends and I escaped from our quiet small town of Chester and made our way to Halifax for a long weekend in the city. We walked the streets and found the chill to the summer night sky igniting our pace, so that our brisk walk had us covering twenty blocks before we knew it. I was looking around in all directions absorbing the energy from people walking by. I found the sights and the sounds of a big city stimulating.

While I was watching a lady almost lose her bonnet to the wind, I collided into my girlfriend Susan who had stopped abruptly. I followed my friend's finger, she was pointing to a sign that read Delphian Den and saying, "I just finished studying a Greek myth about Apollo and Delphi. Let's stop here for a bite to eat." Our brisk walk had exaggerated our appetites, so the group was all in agreement. My friends refer to me as the voice of reason, but before I could point out that it had no windows they had started to enter The Delphian Den.

I was a teenager in 1795 and totally unaware that opening that door cemented my destiny. By stepping into The Delphian Den, I set in stone the legacy of Daniel McGinnis. As I lie here contemplating life, I find it interesting how many doors we blindly walk through from birth to death, and yet most people try to avoid the one threshold we will all inevitably have to cross. I have asked myself on many occasions throughout my lifetime, "If I knew then what I know now, would I walk through the door of the Delphian Den again?" My answer has changed with the seasons of my life, and as I write this during my final winter, I think that I should have "run like hell."

My mind cast a line that reached through decades, and I remembered. Having no clue of the consequences to come, I followed my friends into the crowded room. Walking through the door, I immediately felt all eyes on us. At the time I was thinking we must be a sight for sore eyes with our wind-blown hair and sweaters askew, but now I realize that we were four young and beautiful women in a room full of men. I spotted four chairs and wanted to blend into the furniture, but Beth had already struck up a conversation with a gentleman near the entrance. Two more men approached us and started talking. As I was about to answer their question, I found myself abruptly whisked away. I would love to relive that moment in time, because I am not entirely sure how I got turned around in an instant. I know I was standing looking in one direction, and in one fluid motion that felt like dancing, my feet lifted off the ground and gently landed with me looking in the opposite direction.

I remember clearly, the giddy feeling like it was yesterday, looking up into Donald's eyes as he said, "If anyone in this room is going to flirt with you, it is going to be me." We sat and talked for hours and discovered we were all practically neighbors. How uncanny that we lived a stone's throw across the bay from each other and came to meet in a crowded city. I found it questionable that this striking man could have lived nearby and gone unnoticed, but he seemed to be knowledgeable about Oak Island and I chose to believe him.

After dinner Don walked us back to our guesthouse. He was quite chivalrous and charming. He stared straight at me with his penetrating green eyes, as he spoke to all of us, "I will be at your door at 0900 hours to deliver you ladies safely back to Chester." We all said, "Yes, sir," even though our original plan was to stay the full weekend in Halifax. We shut the door giggling like schoolgirls, which I guess we were.

As soon as the door shut, Susan exclaimed, “Barb, he did not take his eyes off of you.” I was well aware of that fact because I did not take my eyes off of him and answered, “He’s so handsome, I couldn’t take my eyes off of him either.” The girls all chimed in, “Ew, why do you like older men?” I laughed, “They are more interesting than the boys we know that have never even left Chester, and Don has seen so much of the world.” We sat up talking all night long, and that was our excuse for not being ready at nine sharp.

We should have guessed that with his military background, he would be on schedule, but the thought did not cross any of our minds. When we arrived at the carriage, Donald stated, “You ladies need a firm lesson in punctuality.” I handed him a cheese biscuit, and when I came up from my curtsy I noticed a slight smile at the corner of his lips.

It was a long cold ride, but I sat atop with Donald the entire way, just so I could listen to his every word. His stories were so interesting and his accent made it all sound so worldly. He painted word pictures so well that I felt I had seen distant lands, even though Halifax was the furthest I had ever been from the town I was born and raised in. His life was so full, in thirty-something years he had lived in Europe and three different states. I soaked up every word until the carriage halted in front of my home.

Needless to say that I was more than slightly shocked when, after introducing Donald to my parents, he proceeded to ask for my hand in marriage. My parents immediately looked at me, asking with their eyes if a transgression had occurred. My father, Henry, voiced his and Cath's concern, "Is there a need for this marriage?"
I was too surprised to acknowledge their question and was thinking only, "why would such a worldly man with a lovely accent be interested in me?"

Donald answered for me, "No, sir." And he turned to address my mother, bowing slightly and said, "My intentions are pure." We sat in the parlor and talked for a time, and my parents were so enamored with Donald that they gave us their blessing. My thoughts were spinning rapidly; jumping from total admiration to love, from love to marriage, all in a single evening. The ideas rolled around in my head, random thoughts popping in and out of view; suffice it to say that I did not sleep well that night.

I was tired the next day when we began our new life together. Donald was excited to take me to the beginnings of a home he started on Oak Island, but I was adamantly opposed to getting in a boat and said I had no interest in leaving the mainland. My parents had offered last night to buy us a plot of land, so that I would not have to live on an island. To say I was quite relieved is an understatement. My voice of reason chimed in wondering why anyone would want to make life so difficult when life itself is hard enough. I could not imagine having to take a boat ride to go shopping or to visit my family and was very grateful to my parents that I did not have to.

Don became intent on searching for the ideal plot of land that would please me, so we started at dawn and went all the way to dusk. We spent the next week adhering to the same daily itinerary, while travelling all around Lunenburg County looking for a homestead. It was an incredibly romantic time, getting to know him as each deliciously warm day carried a deeper chill. I don't remember what I had to say about myself, but I do remember every word Donald shared on the long carriage rides. His hands were beautiful as they held the reins with relaxed control, everything about him was nothing short of spectacular. He was a fantastic storyteller and as our week culminated, I felt as if I had personally travelled across the Atlantic Ocean, even though that is something that I would never do.

As our search produced nothing of value, Don reminded me that he had a plot of land on Oak Island but I continued to steer us away from the sea. I wondered if he had ever seen a nor'easter, and then thought to myself that he probably had

experienced one out on the open ocean. I had a strange thought that maybe because he had already lived through many dangers and had survived, that could somehow transfer to me and apply a new sense of bravery. This crazy idea gave me a moment of false bravado during which I conceded to look at his homestead. Even though I had agreed, it was still difficult for him to coax me into the tiny skiff.
Donald said, "You have nothing to fear." As he steadied the bow of the boat with one hand and held my hand with his other. I had absolutely no desire to step foot on that boat, my internal voice of reason alerted me that just because he survived so many trials does not in any way ensure that I will not sink. A wave came and wet my shoes and the edges of my skirt, and I stamped my foot in the sand saying, "This is totally unnecessary! Seriously, you cannot find a piece of land you like on the mainland?"

He threw his head back and laughed out loud, while letting go of the boat he scooped me in his arms and gently placed me in the stern of the boat. Before I knew it we were underway, and I sat there wondering how he changed everything so quickly. As Don rowed, he proceeded to answer like he had heard my unasked question, "There have been many times in my life that I felt afraid and the best way to escape the immobilizing grip of fear, is to just do it quickly." He was keeping the boat very steady and asked,

"Now Barb, is this really so bad? Can you get past the things that scare you and conquer your fear?"

I thought not, and crossed my arms in front of my chest and answered, "I have seen people after they have drowned." As I let that sobering fact sink in, I turned my head away for effect and was relieved to see the water was shallow again. When we were just a few feet from the island I turned back to look him in the eye, while I let out a dramatic sigh of relief that we made it.

He gave me an understanding nod but with a strong Scottish accent said, "my father would say, you're a long time deid."

I probably looked mortified when I asked, "Did you say dead? Why would your father say that?"

Donald stood on the beach wearing the most beautiful smile. I guessed that he was remembering his dad when he spoke, "Dadaidh was just sharing a Scottish saying that points out the fact that once you are dead, no one knows what type of experiences can be felt, so experience life while you are able."

Those words inspired me to decline his outstretched hand, and I bravely splashed my foot in the water, as I took my first step onto Oak Island. I had seen this land in the distance all my life, yet I had never been. Even from a distance, its natural beauty was intriguing and different from the other 300 plus islands in Mahone Bay. Years ago I had chosen to paint this island because the Oak trees that rose made the island look surreal, especially in the fall when the bright red canopy lit up the sky. I tried to capture the look on canvas, but did not do it justice. I found it impossible to portray the size of the hundred foot tall pine trees and even taller majestic oak trees that were towering above.

As magical as it felt and unique as it appeared, I am still not sure how he talked me into living on an island. But Donald led the way and I followed. We were married in the town of Chester on September 8, 1795. During our ceremony the priest stated my baptized name first and switched it from Barbara Mary to Mary Barbara, and the priest also changed Donald to the biblical name of Daniel.

My new husband insisted that we honor the Priest and he started calling me Mary, even though I did not answer the first few weeks he called my name. I was relieved that both his names started with the letter D, so he did not notice when I'd catch myself messing up. It was just the first of many mistakes and the beginning of many miraculous moments that all wove together to become the story of our life on Oak Island…

This Is Not THE END

Because We WILL See Each Other Again!

Made in the USA
Lexington, KY
13 March 2019